# INTERNATIONAL BILLIONAIRES

*Life is a game of power and pleasure.*
*And these men play to win!*

Let Modern™ Romance take you on a jet-set journey
to meet eight male wonders of the world.
From rich tycoons to royal playboys—
they're red-hot and ruthless!

International Billionaires coming in 2009

8 volumes in all to collect!

**Dear Reader**

I was thrilled to be asked to write one in a series of books centring around the exciting world of International Rugby. My home, Ireland, is bursting with Rugby pride and prowess. The backdrop of Six Nations fever certainly helped me to envisage the single-minded pursuit of an arrogant French hero intent on the seduction of my vulnerable, yet strong Irish heroine!

The game, to me, represents earthy competition and raw sport at its most base and primal level—heady stuff, and very evocative of passion and attraction.

Recently the matches have been played out in the impressive Dublin ground of Croke Park, and that's where I've set the opening of my story. As of 2010, though, the game will return to its home ground of Lansdowne Road, which is currently being refurbished to international standards.

When it came to research—well, let's just say that it was no hardship to sit and watch the Six Nations in preparation. I have to confess while watching France v Italy my focus on the rules of the game did wander a little from time to time.

I hope that you enjoy reading Alana and Pascal's story as much as I enjoyed the process of writing it...

Happy reading!

*Abby*

# THE FRENCH TYCOON'S PREGNANT MISTRESS

BY
ABBY GREEN

MILLS & BOON®
*Pure reading pleasure*™

First published in Great Britain 2009
Harlequin Mills & Boon Limited,
Eton House, 18-24 Paradise Road, Richmond, Surrey TW9 1SR

© Abby Green 2009


ISBN: 978 0 263 20714 9

Set in Times Roman 1
07-0209-56884

Printed and bound in Great Britain
by CPI Antony Rowe, Chippenham, Wiltshire

**Abby Green** got hooked on Mills & Boon romances while still in her teens, when she stumbled across one belonging to her grandmother, in the west of Ireland. After many years of reading them voraciously, she sat down one day and gave it a go herself. Happily, after a few failed attempts, her first manuscript was accepted. Abby works freelance in the Film and TV industry but thankfully the 4 a.m. starts and stresses of dealing with recalcitrant actors are becoming more and more infrequent, leaving more time to write! She loves to hear from readers and you can contact her through her website at www.abby-green.com. She lives and works in Dublin.

# CHAPTER ONE

'WITH a nail-biting finish like that, I think we can safely say that this tournament is wide-open and set to be one of the most exciting yet. This is Alana Cusack, reporting live from Croke Park. Back to you in the studio, Brian.'

Alana kept the smile pasted on her face until she could hear the chatter die away in her earpiece and then handed her microphone to her assistant, Aisling, with relief once she knew she was off air. She avoided looking to where she knew the man was still standing, his shoulder propped nonchalantly against the wall, hands in the pockets of his dark trousers, underneath a black overcoat with the collar turned up. He'd been talking to one of the French players, but now he was alone again.

He was watching her. And he'd been watching her all through the Six Nations match between Ireland and France. He'd unsettled her and he'd distracted her. And she didn't know why.

That was a lie; she knew exactly why. He was dark and brooding, and so gorgeous that when she'd first locked eyes with him, quite by accident, it had felt as though someone had just punched her in the stomach. There had been an instant tug of recognition and something very alien and disconcerting. Certainly something that no other man had ever made her feel.

Not even her husband.

The tug had been so strong that she'd felt herself smiling and raising a quizzical brow, but then she'd seen an unmistakably mocking glint in his dark eyes. Of course, she didn't know him; she'd never seen his long, hard-boned face before, had never seen that mouth, which even to look at from where she sat, had the most amazingly sensuous lips. Immediately she'd felt herself flushing with embarrassment at her reaction to him.

He had to be French, as he shared the quintessential good looks of so many of the crowd today, quite exotically different from the more pale-skinned home crowd of Irish supporters. And he'd been sitting in the seats reserved for VIP's, situated just below the press area. He looked like a VIP. She'd only had to look once to know that he effortlessly stood out from the rest of the crowd. But her gaze had been inexorably drawn to him again and again, and to her utter ongoing mortification their eyes had met more than once. When he'd stood intermittently with the crowd during a try or a conversion, he'd stood taller and broader than any of the men around him—and in a crowd full of rugby supporters, that was something.

Yet was he waiting now because he thought that she'd been giving him some sort of come-on? Everything in Alana clammed up and rejected that thought. She would never be so blatant.

'Do you need a lift, Alana?' Aisling and the others had finished packing up, and Derek the cameraman was looking at her. Suddenly she felt very flustered. She didn't *get* flustered. She was often teased for appearing cool, calm and collected at all times.

'No,' she answered quickly, aware that the stranger had moved out of her peripheral vision. A sense of panic threatened her—that he might be right behind her, waiting for her. 'I have to go to a family dinner later, so I have my car here.'

'So no glitzy after-party to see the French celebrating for you, then?'

She mock-grimaced, secretly relieved that she had an excuse. 'I'll only have time to stop in to show my face on my way, just to keep Rory happy.'

He shrugged and was about to walk away after Aisling and the other assistant, with their small amount of gear, when he stopped and turned again, distracting Alana.

'Good reporting today, kid.'

Pleasure rushed through her. This was so important to her; Derek was practically a veteran of TV. She'd been slogging for a long time to get a modicum of respect. She smiled. 'Thanks, Derek. I really appreciate that.'

He winked at her and turned to walk away again. With the fizz of pleasure staying in her chest, she checked around for anything left behind and made to follow the others, before stopping and cursing as she remembered that her laptop and notebook were back in the press seats.

Derek's words were forgotten when that prickling awareness came back. She turned around with her heart beating hard, fully expecting to see the man again. She had a curiously insincere feeling of relief when he wasn't there. He'd obviously gone, bored with waiting around. Taking the lift back up to the upper level, she told herself to stop being ridiculous, that she'd merely imagined that they'd had some kind of silent communication…

He thought he'd missed her when he'd gone to look at the pitch for a moment, and he didn't like the momentary sense of panic that thought had generated.

But she was still here.

Now Pascal Lévêque stood back with arms folded and surveyed the enticing sight in front of him. A very shapely bottom was raised in the air, encased in the tight confines of a pencil skirt. Its owner was currently bending over, hauling a bag out from under a seat. His eyes drifted down. Long, slim legs were momentarily bent and now straightened to their full length—which was *long*, all the way from slim, neat ankles right up to gently flaring hips which tapered into a neat waist. He wondered if she was wearing stockings, and that thought had a forceful effect on the blood in his veins.

He wondered, too, then, what it was about her that had kept him looking, that had kept him here, when he should have long gone. What was it that had kept drawing his eye back again and again, uncharacteristically taking his attention away from the riveting match?

*Neat.*

That was it. She was neat. Right from her starchy, buttoned-up stripey shirt complete with tie, down to her sensible court-shoes and shiny, straight hair neatly tucked behind her ears, a side parting to the left. It was tied back in a small ponytail, but he could well imagine that if let loose, it would fall ever so neatly into a straight shoulder-length bob, framing her face. And since when had he been into *neat*? He was famously into seductive, sensual women, women who poured their beautiful, curvaceous bodies into clothes and dresses designed to fire the imagination and ignite the senses. Women who weren't afraid to entice and beguile, using all their powerful charms for his pleasure.

She was shrugging into a long, black overcoat now, hiding herself, and bizarrely, he felt all at once irritated, inflamed and perplexed. What the hell was he doing, practically slavering over some vacuous TV dolly bird? He knew that any second now she'd turn round, and he'd see that up close her face wasn't half as alluring as he'd imagined it to be from a distance: with a healthy glow, full, glossy lips and doe-shaped eyes under dark brows which contrasted with her strawberry-blonde hair.

No; she'd turn round and he'd see that she was caked in orange make-up. Her eyes would flare with recognition— hadn't she already recognised him earlier, and given him those enticingly shy looks? And then he'd be caught. He was already trying to think up something to excuse his very out-of-character behaviour when she did turn round. He opened his mouth and suddenly his mind went blank.

Alana had no warning for what or who faced her. That gorgeous, brooding stranger was right in front of her. Just feet away. Looking at her. They were standing alone in an eighty-thousand-seat stadium, but to Alana in that moment it shrank to the four square feet surrounding them. And it was then that she had to acknowledge that the prickling awareness she'd been dismissing had just exploded into full-on shock. The blood seemed to thicken in her veins; her heart pounded again in recognition of some base appreciation of his very masculinity.

He stood with his head tilted back, hands in the pockets of his trousers. His coat emphasised his broad shoulders, the olive tone of his skin. But it was his eyes that she couldn't take her own shocked gaze from. They were wide, dark, intelligent and full of something so hot and brazenly sensual that she felt breathless.

Her hands gripped her notebooks close to her chest, and she was absurdly relieved that she was wearing a long coat, feeling very strangely that this man could somehow see underneath, as if with just a look he could make her clothes melt away. She shook her head, unaware of what she was doing, and to her intense relief, she found her voice.

'Excuse me, can I help you? Are you looking for someone?' Since when had her voice taken on the huskily seductive tones of a jazz singer? Even though they were alone, Alana felt no sense of fear. Her sense of fear came from an entirely different direction.

'You were looking at me.'

Pascal winced inwardly at the accusing tone of his voice and the baldness of his statement, but he was still reeling from coming face to face with her. His recent assumption that she would prove to be entirely unalluring was blasted to smithereens. She was all at once pale and glowing. Dewy. Cheeks flushed red from the cold breeze...or something else? That thought had blood rushing southward with an unwelcome lack of control. Her eyes were a unique shade of light green. Her lips were full and soft, not covered in glossy gloop. He'd never seen anyone so naturally beguiling.

'Excuse me?' Alana welcomed the righteous indignation that flowed through her, and told herself it wasn't adrenaline. But since when had righteous indignation made her shake? She'd been right; he was obviously just a tourist looking for a little fun. He'd misconstrued her meaning when she'd smiled at him. Well, she wasn't on the market for that sort of thing.

'From what I recall you were doing a fair amount of looking yourself.' She hitched up her chin. 'I thought I recognised you, but I was wrong, so forgive me if I led you to believe that something more was on offer. Now, if you'll excuse me, I have work to get back to.'

The man smiled, revealing gleaming, strong white teeth, and Alana felt momentarily dizzy. 'I am well aware that you are working, after all, didn't I just see you interviewing Ireland's manager? I was making an observation, that's all. And you were looking at me.'

'No more than you were looking at me.' She desperately tried to claw back some semblance of control.

He rocked back on his heels and a different light came into his eyes. An altogether more dangerous light. And Alana could see that she was effectively trapped. The space between the seats was far too narrow for her to even attempt to push past him, and the only alternative would be to jump into the next aisle—far too unladylike and desperate. And, in the skirt she was wearing, impossible.

Alana felt unbelievably threatened. She called up her best brisk manner and hitched her laptop-bag strap higher on her shoulder, hoping he'd take the hint. 'This conversation is getting us nowhere. Now, really, I have to get back to my office, and I'm sure you have somewhere far more exciting to be.'

After a long, intense moment, to her utter relief, he stepped back and indicated with his arm that she should precede him out of the row of seats that led into the press area. Alana gritted her teeth and walked past, but, even though she tried to arch her whole body away as she moved past him, she was aware of his height which had to be at least six foot four, the sheer breadth of him and an enticingly musky smell.

The smell of *sex*.

Oh God, what was wrong with her? Since when had she ever thought she could smell *sex*? And since when had she even been aware of what it smelt like? She felt weak in the pit of her stomach, but thankfully she was now past him and hurrying back up the main steps to the lift, which would bring her down to ground level and back to reality.

Her silent prayers weren't answered when she felt his presence beside her, yet he said nothing as the lift doors opened. When he stepped in with her, Alana punched the button, silently pleading for the journey down to be quick. It was excruciatingly intense, sharing the small confined space, and she practically bolted as soon as the lift juddered to a halt and the doors opened. As she walked towards the main gates at the back of the stand, Alana could see her car parked on the road outside. And then she heard his steps stop behind her.

Of course, he'd kept up with her effortlessly; she had the unsettling feeling that she was on a tight leash. He was like a predator indulging his prey, not moving in for the kill just yet. And knowing that, against all rational thought in her head, Alana stopped, too, and turned round. Her heart was still pounding from the close proximity in the lift, and she just realised then that she must have held her breath the whole way down.

He was looking at her with those intense eyes. And then he said, 'Actually, I do have somewhere more exciting to be. Maybe you'd care to join me?'

The full effect of his accent washed through her now; it was as if she'd blocked it out when she'd first heard him speak, having been too much to cope with along with everything else. He was absolutely devastating, and he *was* coming on to her. Alana couldn't believe it. She knew perfectly well she was nothing special; she looked like a million other girls. What on earth could this man want with her? Anyone could see he was in another league. Alarm bells rang, loud and insistently.

She shook her head and started backing away towards the gate and her car, but the physical pull to stay in this man's orbit was something she had to actively fight against. Simultaneously a sleek, dark Lexus pulled up beside them. Clearly his car—his chauffeur-driven car—which had of course been parked here in the VIP parking area.

She was shaking her head. 'I'm sorry, Mr…?'

'Lévêque.'

'Mr Lévêque.' Even his name sounded sexy—purposeful. Important. 'I have to get back to work.' She repeated it then, as if to drive a point home. 'This is work for me. Enjoy your weekend in Dublin. There are plenty of other women out there.' *Who won't be stupid enough to walk away*, the voice mocked her. But as she finally turned and walked towards her car she told herself she was glad. He hadn't looked put out; he hadn't even tried to get her to change her mind. He was just a rich tourist over for the match. And she knew all about sports supporters. She used to be part of that crowd, used to *be* a professional supporter. Not any more.

Pascal refused to give in to the desire to look to where she was getting into her car as his own swept past and away from the stadium. He couldn't really believe that she'd refused him. A woman hadn't walked away from him since…he couldn't remember when. His mouth thinned. She was right: there were plenty of other women out there. She really wasn't anything special.

So why was it that all he could see were those invitingly soft lips? And those huge, green eyes, full of changing depths? And that alluring body in its veritable uniform that made his hands itch to rip it off and see what it hid?

He was bored. That was it. And he'd been without a lover for some weeks. He was going to a party tonight. If all he was looking for was a quick lay, then he'd get it in spades.

Feeling his equilibrium start to settle again was a welcome relief, because it hadn't been normal since he'd laid eyes on her. He settled back and relaxed. And then promptly tensed again, all recent justifications out the window. He hadn't got her name. And he didn't even know if she was married. He couldn't remember seeing a ring, but now it glared at him. That *had* to be it. Equanimity rushed through him again. This time he firmly cast her out of his head as a weird, momentary diversion and looked forward to the fast-approaching evening and the promise of fulfilment that was now a dull, throbbing ache in his body.

'Alana, you can't leave yet.'

'But, Rory, I've got to get home, it's my brother's fortieth.'

Her boss ignored her and pulled her firmly by the hand, back into the throng of people she'd just battled her way through to get out. She rolled her eyes in exasperation.

'Alana, you have to meet him, you're interviewing him tomorrow. He rang in person after the match, specifically asking for you—must have seen you reporting or something, but who cares? Do you have any idea what a coup this is? He's an important sponsor of the Six Nations…famously reclusive… billionaire.'

Alana was getting bumped and bashed by people along the way as she struggled to keep up with her hyper TV-boss. She couldn't hear half of what he was saying. Something about an interview? That was nothing unusual; she did interviews most days. Why was he making such a big deal about this one? She cast a quick, worried look at her watch on the wrist not held captive by Rory. The surprise party would be starting in half an hour, and it would take her that to get out to her parents' house in Foxrock. If she missed the start of it, her life wouldn't be worth living.

Then Rory stopped abruptly and she careened into him. He turned and gave her a worried once-over. 'You'll do; it's a pity you're not more dressed up, you know, Alana, you could have made more of an effort. Really.' His mouth pursed in disapproval.

Irritation rankled; all too frequently people seemed to expect her to be what she had been—before. 'Rory, I'm dressed for a family party, remember? Not the French team's celebrations.'

Which she had to privately admit now were something else. Clearly someone had a lot of money to spend. They were taking place in the lavish ballroom of the Four Seasons hotel just on the outskirts of Dublin city-centre. She wasn't dressed in the glittering half-sheath dresses that most of the women seemed to be sporting, but she was perfectly respectable. And she preferred it that way. She had too many uncomfortable memories of being paraded in fashions that had been too tight, too small, too *everything*. And not her. She knew she went out of her way in situations like this to draw the line between the woman she had been and the woman she was now.

Rory looked over her head, tensed visibly and then looked back, taking her shoulders as if she were a child. 'He's just arrived. Now, I can't impress upon you how important this man is. Apart from his role in the Six Nations, he's the CEO of one of the biggest banks in the world. I'll introduce you and then you can go, OK? No doubt he's got bigger fish to fry tonight than meeting you, anyway.'

Rory grabbed her hand again, and before Alana could say anything, he was leading her over to where a man stood with his black-suited back to them, surrounded by obviously fawning people and a couple of scantily dressed women. And suddenly Alana's legs turned to jelly. Even before they reached him she felt her heart start to pound in recognition. It got about a million times worse when Rory hissed in her ear, 'His name is Lévêque. Pascal Lévêque.'

'I believe I saw you covering the match earlier, no?' He said this innocently with that deeply sexy voice, as if they'd never met.

For the second time that day Alana looked up into those eyes. Those eyes that she hadn't been able to get out of her head. Her mouth turned dry, her hands clammy. Her reaction was alarming; she'd sworn off all men, and had no time for frivolous flirtations, and she couldn't understand why this man was having such an extreme effect on her. Other men flirted with her and asked her out, and she dismissed them with barely a ripple of acknowledgement or reaction. But this was different. And she'd known it from the moment she had met him, which was why she'd all but run.

Silence lengthened, and Rory nudged her discreetly but painfully. Automatically Alana held out a hand. She spoke on autopilot. 'Yes. Yes, you did.'

Pascal Lévêque then took her hand in his much larger one, but instead of shaking it he bent his head, his eyes never leaving hers. Alana saw what he was going to do as if in slow motion, but still the feel of his mouth on the back of her cool hand sent shockwaves through her entire body. Immediately she tried to pull her hand away, but he wouldn't let her go. He straightened slowly. She felt his index finger uncurl to caress the point under the wrist where her pulse beat fast, and then he let her hand go. The gesture was fleeting but utterly earth-shattering.

He broke their eye contact, leaving Alana feeling curiously deflated, and with a brief, succinct question Rory left, muttering something about getting drinks. The rest of the crowd the man had been talking to melted away too. He turned back, fixing on her with that intense gaze again.

'You've had time to change, I see. Tell me, is this still classed as work?'

Alana bristled. Hot, burning irritation was rising. 'Of course I changed—it's a party. And, yes, this is still work.'

His eyes swept down, taking in what she knew to be a perfectly suitable albeit very unexciting dress. It was a black shift, high-necked and under a matching jacket. Unrevealing.

'You've changed, too,' she pointed out, feeling ridiculously self-conscious. But, whereas she felt sure she merged into the background, he was managing to stand out in a crowd of identically dressed men in a traditional black tuxedo, white shirt and black bow tie.

His eyes met hers again. 'Don't you want to take off your coat? It's warm in here.'

*Warm!*

She could feel a trickle of sweat roll down between her breasts as if his words had just turned the room into a sauna. 'No, I'm fine.' But all at once the jacket which had felt positively lightweight now felt like a bear skin. To be confronted with him up close and personal was overwhelming. Her eyes wanted to look their fill of his broad, lean body, wanted to rest and dwell and see if he filled out his suit as well as she suspected he did. Who was she kidding? As well as she *knew* he did. She didn't have to look to feel the latent power of his taut body envelop her in waves.

Before she knew what she was doing, she felt her hand come up in a telling gesture to smooth her hair behind her ear. It was a nervous habit. His eyes narrowed and followed her movement, and Alana flushed. Damn. She did not want to look like she was in any way aware of him.

A smile quirked his mouth. 'Your hair is perfectly…tidy.'

Was he laughing at her? And then she remembered what Rory had said. She glared up at him. Her hand dropped. 'Is it true that you requested me for this interview?'

He shrugged nonchalantly. 'It's tiresome, but every now and then I have to give in to press demands. So, yes, I requested you…in the hope that, perhaps with you asking the questions, it would prove a more diverting experience than I'm used to.'

His eyes were hot and sensual. Everything professional in her reacted to his dismissive and high-handed manner. She smiled sweetly, and something treacherous ignited in her belly when she saw a flare of something in his eyes. She ignored her body's response. 'Mr Lévêque. If you think that just because I'm a woman I'm going to confine my questions to what your favourite colour might be, then you're sadly mistaken.' At that moment she made a mental note to stay up all night if she had to, to research this man.

His eyes narrowed and cooled, and she shivered slightly.

'And if you think that because you're a woman I would dismiss your ability on that basis alone, then you are much mistaken. Any interest I have in you as far as the interview goes *is* purely professional. I've had your work investigated, and you impressed me.'

Alana was completely taken aback, and immediately felt like apologising. But, looking up at him now, she felt that cool wind still washing over her. She could almost believe that she had imagined his hot look of just moments ago. That she had imagined everything leading up to this point. She had an uncanny prescience of what it would be like to be this man's enemy.

'Well, I'm… That is, I hadn't thought that—'

He cut off her inarticulate attempt to apologise. 'Like I said, my interest in you is purely professional…as far as the interview goes. However…' He stopped and moved closer. The air around them changed in a heartbeat. Became charged.

Alana sucked in a breath. His eyes were hot again, making her feel very disorientated.

'I can't promise that my interest doesn't extend beyond the professional.'

As with earlier in the stadium, Alana felt as though the huge, packed ballroom had just shrunk around them. Adrenaline pumped through her along with the desire to flee.

'Mr Lévêque. I'm very sorry, but you see—'

'Are you married?' he asked so quickly and abruptly that Alana was stunned.

'Yes,' she answered automatically, and saw something dark flash across his face. And then she stepped back and shook her head. What was this man doing to her brain? 'No. I mean I am, I *was*, married.' She bit her lip and looked out to the room briefly, desperately willing Rory to come back and interrupt them. She looked back up at Pascal with the utmost reluctance. His eyes glittered, and a muscle twitched in his jaw. She wondered how they'd got onto such personal territory so quickly, and then his words came back: *I can't promise that my interest doesn't extend beyond the professional.*

A whole host of emotions and memories was threatening to

consume her. And the fact that she was here, in an environment so evocative of her past, was quickly becoming claustrophobic. She took a breath, deeply resenting that he was making her talk about this. 'I *was* married. My husband died eighteen months ago.'

Pascal opened his mouth as if to say something, and Alana was already tensing in anticipation. But her prayers had been heard, and Rory bounded up at that moment with drinks. He thrust a glass of champagne at Alana before handing what looked like a whiskey to Pascal. And then panic struck. She put the glass on a nearby table, some of the champagne sloshing out over the rim.

She opened her bag to pull her phone out. Ten missed calls. She groaned, 'I am in *so* much trouble.'

She turned to Rory. 'I have to go.' She looked at Pascal briefly, welcoming the feeling of panic which was distracting her from his overpowering presence.

'I'm sorry, but I'm already late for another engagement.'

She started backing away, valiantly ignoring Rory's none-too-subtle facial expressions. She bumped into someone and apologised. She felt her hair come loose from its sleek chignon and pushed it behind her ear. She was literally coming apart.

'It was nice to…meet you, Mr Lévêque. I look forward to the interview.' *Liar.* He just watched her, a small, enigmatic smile playing around that hard mouth, and stuck one hand deep into a pocket. Alana could already see women hovering, ready to move back in again, and something curdled in her stomach.

'Me, too,' he said softly, and lifted his glass like a salute— or a threat. '*Á demain*, Alana.' *Till tomorrow.*

It was disconcerting to say the least to try and conduct a co-herent conversation while the remnants of the hottest lust he'd ever experienced still washed through his body in waves. Even the welcome knowledge that she wasn't married failed now to impinge on his racing mind. He was still trying to clamp down the intensely urgent desire to know exactly whom she had gone to meet and where. Was it a date?

'So, what made you decide to ask for Alana Cusack to interview you?' Her boss, Rory Hogan, the head of the sports division of the national TV channel, laughed nervously. He was beginning to intensely irritate Pascal with his obsequious behaviour—and also by drawing his attention to the uncomfortable fact that, in the space of the short car journey earlier, Pascal had gone from dismissing Alana Cusack from his head to making a series of calls to find out exactly who she was, and then requesting her for his interview the next day.

Following an instinct, he decided not to dismiss this man straight away. 'I decided to use her because she's the best reporter you've got, of course.'

Rory's flushed face got even more flushed. 'Well, thank you. Yes, she is good. In fact, she's rather surprised us all.' The other man looked round for a second and then moved closer. Pascal fought against taking a step back; Rory was becoming progressively more drunk.

'The thing is, you see, she was only given a chance because of who she is.'

Pascal's interest sharpened. He injected a tone of bored uninterest into his voice. 'What do you mean?'

Rory laughed and waved an arm around. 'See all these women hanging on?'

Pascal didn't have to look; they were practically nipping at his heels. His lip curled with distaste. Situations like this always attracted a certain kind of woman—eager for marriage to a millionaire sportsman, and the platinum-credit-card lifestyle his wages could afford. The women who had achieved that status lorded it over the ones who hadn't, but it didn't make them any less predatory.

'Well, she was one of them. The queen of them, in fact. Y'see, she was married to Ryan O'Connor.'

Pascal sucked in a breath, shocked despite himself. Even he had heard of the legendary Irish soccer-player. That knowledge fought with the mental image of Alana in front of him just now, in that unrevealing black dress that had covered her from neck to knee, her hair as tidy and smooth as it had been earlier.

Rory was on a roll now. 'When they got married, it was the biggest wedding in Ireland for years. The first big celebrity-wedding. The Irish football team were having back-to-back wins. Alana was seen as their lucky mascot; she went to all the matches. It was an idyllic marriage, a great time…and then she wrecked it all.' Rory flushed. 'Well, I mean, I know she's not personally responsible, but—'

'What do you mean?' Pascal was rapidly trying to remember what he knew about Ryan O'Connor, still slightly stunned at what Alana's boss was revealing.

'Well, she threw him out, didn't she? For no good reason. And Ryan went off the rails. Ireland's luck ran out, and then he died in that helicopter crash just days before the divorce was through. We ended up giving her a job because she was unbelievably persistent, and she knows sports inside out. It's in her blood; her father played rugby for Ireland.'

Pascal was still trying to reconcile the image he had of Alana with the women around him in their tiny dresses that left little to the imagination. And yet, he could see her now as she'd been backing away just moments ago; she'd been flushed in the face, and a lock of hair had been coming loose. It had been that which had sent his lust levels off the scale. He'd had a tantalising glimpse of her coming undone, of something *hot* beneath that über-cool surface.

But the thought that she had been one of those women made everything in him contract with disgust. Yet she certainly hadn't been flirting with him, despite knowing who he was. Unless it was just a tactic. In which case, he vowed to himself now, he'd play with her to see how far she was willing to go and walk away when he'd had enough. One thing was for certain—he wanted to seduce her with an urgency that was fast precluding anything else.

The next day Alana looked at herself in the mirror of the ladies toilet at work. Nervously, and hating herself for feeling nervous, she smoothed her already smooth hair. She'd tied it back in its usual style for work, and now tucked it firmly behind her ears. She leant close to check her make-up. She'd had to put slightly more on than usual today to cover the circles under her eyes. She'd arrived home late last night, and had then stayed up researching as much information about Pascal Lévêque as she could.

The fact that she hadn't had to stay up long said it all. He rarely gave interviews; the last one had been at least two years previously. He was the CEO of Banque Lévêque, and had reached that exalted position at a ridiculously young age. Now in his mid-to-late thirties, he had brought a conglomerate of smaller archaic banks kicking and screaming into the twenty-first century, turning them into Banque Lévêque and making it one of the most influential financial institutions in the world.

Alana saw the flush on her cheeks and scrambled for some powder to try and disguise it. There had been little on his childhood or family, just one line to say that he'd been born in the suburbs of Paris to an unwed mother. Nothing about his father.

Her mouth twisted cynically. She wouldn't have been surprised in the slightest to learn that he was married. From her experience, the holy sanctity of marriage was a positive incitement for men to play away. She stopped trying to calm her hectic colour down; it was useless, and if she put any more make-up on, she'd look like a clown. She met her own eyes and didn't like the glitter she saw.

The wealth of information she'd found on his personal life—quite at odds with the paucity of information on his family or professional life—had put paid to the suspicion that he could be married. Picture after picture of stunning beauties on his arm abounded on the Internet. It would appear that he'd courted and fêted an indecent amount of the world's most renowned actresses, models and it-girls. However, no woman ever seemed to appear more than twice.

The man was obviously a serial seducer, a connoisseur of women. A playboy with a capital *P*. And Alana Cusack, from a nice, comfortable, unremarkable middle-class background, with a relatively attractive face and body, was not in his league. Not even close.

He was rich. He was powerful. He was successful. He played to win. He was the very epitome of everything she'd vowed never to let into her life again. She packed up her make-up things and gave herself a quick once-over. Her dark-navy trouser suit, and cream silk-shirt buttoned up as high as it would go, screamed *professional*. She adjusted the string of *faux* pearls around her neck. With any luck he'd have met and seduced one of the many women at the party last night, and not even remember the fact that he'd shown any interest in her.

'Let's get started, shall we?'

Alana spoke briskly, and barely glanced up from her notes when Pascal was shown into the studio. But she felt the air contract, the energy shift. The excitement was tangible. She hadn't even experienced this level of palpable charisma from some of the world's most famous sportsmen. She'd been given a thorough briefing from an attendant PR-person not to stray into personal territory, and above all, not to ask him about relationships with women. As if she even wanted to go there.

She felt rather than saw him sit down opposite her. She could hear the clatter of people getting ready around them with lights and the camera. Derek was with her again today, and he said now, 'Just a couple of minutes; I need to check the lights again.' Alana muttered something, feeling absurdly irritated. She just wanted to get this over with.

'Late night last night?'

She looked up quickly and glanced round to see if anyone had heard. No one appeared to have. She hated the intimate tone he'd used, as if drawing her into some kind of dialogue that existed just between them. It was less than twenty-four hours since she'd met him in the first place. She *had* to nip this in the bud. She looked at him steadily, ignoring the shockwaves running through her body at seeing him again.

'No.' She was frosty. 'Not particularly. You?' Why had she asked him that? She could have kicked herself.

He smiled a slow, languorous smile that did all sorts of things to her insides. She gritted her teeth. He was immaculate again today in a dark suit and pale shirt, a silk tie making him look every inch the stupendously successful financier that he was. 'I went to bed early with a cup of hot cocoa and dreamt of you in your buttoned-up suit.'

Before she could react to his comment, his eyes flicked over her in a brazen appraisal. 'A variation on a theme today, I see. Do you have a different suit for every day of the week?'

A molten, heated flush was spreading through Alana like quickfire. She was so incensed that he was already toying with her that she couldn't get words out. They were stuck in her throat.

'OK, Alana, we're ready to go here.'

Derek's voice cut through the fire in her blood. She glared at Pascal for a long moment and struggled to control herself. He hadn't taken his eyes off hers, and now he smiled easily, innocently. With a monumental effort, Alana found her cool poise. And after the first few questions had been asked, and Pascal had answered with easy, incisive intelligence, Alana began to relax. She'd found a system that was working. She just avoided looking at him if at all possible.

And that was working a treat until he said, 'I don't feel like you're really connecting with me.'

She had to look at him then. 'Excuse me?'

His eyes bored into hers, an edge of humour playing around his lips that only she could see. 'I don't feel the connection.'

Alana was very aware of everyone standing around them and looking on with interest. She wanted to get up and walk out, or hit him to get that smug look off his face. 'I'm sorry. How can I help you feel more...connected?'

He gave her an explicit look that spoke volumes, but said innocuously, 'Eye contact would be a help.'

She heard a snigger from one of the crew in the room. A familiar pain lanced her. There was always the reminder that people wanted to see her fail. She smiled benignly. 'Of course.'

Then the interview took on a whole new energy because, now that he was demanding that she make eye contact with him, she couldn't remain immune to the effect he had on her. And he knew it. She struggled through a few more questions, but with each one it felt as though he was sucking her into some kind of vortex. The sensation of an intimate web enmeshing them was becoming too much.

In a desperate bid to drive him back somehow, she deviated from her script, and could sense Rory's tension spike from across the room as she asked the question. 'How did a boy from the suburbs in Paris develop an interest in rugby? Isn't it considered a relatively middle-class game?'

Now she could sense the PR-person tense, but they didn't intervene. Clearly Pascal Lévêque was not someone to be *minded*, unlike other celebrities. He would stay in absolute control of any situation. For the first time, he didn't answer straight away. He just looked at her, and she felt a quiver of fear. He smiled tightly, but it didn't reach his eyes. 'You've done your research.'

Alana just nodded faintly, sorry she'd brought it up now.

But then he answered, 'It was my grandfather.'

'Your grandfather?' She avoided looking down at her notes, but she knew there had been no mention of a grandfather.

He nodded. 'I was sent to the south of France to live with him when I was in my teens.' He shrugged minutely, his eyes still unreadable. 'A teenage boy and the suburbs of Paris isn't a good mix.'

Something in his eyes, his face, made her want to say, 'it's OK; you don't have to answer', and that shocked her, as she never normally shied away from asking tough questions. And she didn't know why this question was generating so many undercurrents. But he continued talking as if the tension between them didn't exist.

'He was hugely involved in league rugby, which is a more parochial version of the game. Very linked to history in France. He instilled in me a love for the game and all its variations.'

Alana had no doubt that she'd touched on something very personal there, and the look in his eyes told her she'd be playing with fire if she continued. All of a sudden, she wanted to play with fire.

'You never considered playing yourself?'

His eyes were positively coal-black and flinty now. He shook his head slightly. 'I discovered that I had a knack for using my head and making money. I prefer to leave rolling around in the dirt to the professionals.'

Alana coloured. Was he making some reference to the fact that *she* was playing dirty, straying into the no-go area of questions into his past? She looked down for a moment to gather herself, and realised that she'd asked all the scripted questions. And then some. She opened her mouth to start thanking him and signing off, when he surprised her by leaning forward.

'Now I have a question for you.'

'You do?' she squeaked. His eyes had changed from black and flinty to brown and…decidedly unflinty.

'Will you have dinner with me tonight?'

Shock and cold, clammy fear slammed into Alana. And then anger that he was asking her in front of an entire crew. The camera was still rolling. She could feel tension snake through the small studio. She tried to laugh it off, but knew she sounded constricted. 'I'm afraid, Mr Lévêque, that my boss doesn't approve of us mixing business with pleasure.'

Rory darted forward, while motioning for the crew to start wrapping up. 'Don't be silly, Alana, this is an entirely unique situation, and I'm sure you'd be only too delighted to show Mr Lévêque gratitude for taking time out of his busy schedule to do this interview.'

Pascal sat back, fully at ease. 'This is my last evening in Dublin. I thought it would be nice to see something of the city. I'd like your company, Alana, but if you insist on saying no, then of course I will understand.'

He stood up and looked down at Rory, straightening his cuffs. 'Can you have the tape of the interview sent over to my hotel? I'm sure it's fine, but I might take the opportunity to approve it fully if I've got some time on my hands.'

In other words, surmised Alana from the tortured look on Rory's pale face at the possibility of losing their biggest scoop to date, Pascal could turn right round and deny them the right to broadcast it. She stood up then, too, and spoke quickly before she could change her mind.

'That won't be necessary, Mr Lévêque. I'd love to have dinner with you. It would be a pleasure.'

# CHAPTER TWO

'I DON'T appreciate being manipulated into situations, Mr Lévêque.'

Pascal looked at Alana's tight-lipped profile from across the other side of the car, and had to subdue the urge to show her exactly how much she might appreciate being manipulated. He knew she felt the simmering tension between them too. At one point during the interview earlier, when she'd had the temerity to dig so deep—too deep—their eyes had stayed locked together for long seconds and he'd read the latent desire in those green depths even if she tried to deny it.

'I prefer to think of it as a gentle nudging.'

She cast a quick look at him and made some kind of inarticulate sound. 'There was nothing gentle about it. Your unspoken threat was very clear, Mr Lévêque—the possibility that you could deny us the right to the interview.'

'Which is something I could still very well do,' he pointed out. As if on cue, Alana turned more fully in her seat. Her eyes spat sparks at him, and he felt a rush of adrenaline through his system. He was so tired of everyone kowtowing to him. But not so this green-eyed witch.

'Is this how you normally conduct your business?' she hissed, mindful of the driver in the front.

He moved closer in an instant, and Alana backed away with a jerk. She could smell his unique scent; already it was becoming familiar to her. One arm ran along the back of the seat, his hand resting far too close to her head, his whole body angled towards her, blocking out any sense of light or the dusky sky outside, creating an intimate cocoon.

'There's nothing businesslike about how you make me feel. And let's just say that I don't normally have to use threats to get a woman to come for dinner with me.'

Alana was reacting to a million things at once, not least of which was her own sense of fatal inevitability. 'No, I saw your track record; it doesn't appear as if you do.'

'Tell me, Alana, why are you so reluctant to go out with me?'

*And why are you so determined?* she wanted to shout. Her hands twisted in her lap, and Pascal caught the movement. Before she could stop him, he had reached down and taken her hands in his, uncurling them, lacing his fingers through with hers. Alana could feel a bizarre mix of soporific delight and a zing of desire so strong that she shook.

'I...don't even like you.'

'You don't know me enough to know if you like me or not. And what's flowing between us right now is nothing to do with *like*.'

*It's lust.* He didn't have to say it.

'I...'

His hands tightened. She could feel his fingers, long and capable, strong, wrapped around hers. She looked down, feeling dazed. She could see her own much paler, smaller hands in a tangle of dark bronze. The image made her think of other parts of her body—limbs enmeshed with his in a tangle of bedlinen. With super-human effort, she pulled her hands free and tucked them well out of his way. She looked at him, and she knew she must look haunted. She felt hunted. Ryan had never reduced her to this carnal level of feeling, and the wound he'd left in her life was still raw. Too raw.

Pascal was close, still crowding her, his eyes roving over her face, but something had changed in the air. He wasn't as intense. He reached out a hand and tucked some hair behind her ear.

'I like your hair down.'

'Look, Pascal…'

He felt something exultant move through him at her unconscious use of his name, and not the awful, prim 'Mr Lévêque'. He dropped his hand. 'Alana, it's just dinner. We'll eat, talk and I'll drop you home.'

At that moment she could feel the car slowing down. They were pulling up outside a world-class restaurant on St Stephen's Green. She seized on his words, his placating tone. She told herself she'd get a taxi home, and then she'd never have to see him again.

She looked at him and nodded jerkily. 'OK.'

Alana was burningly aware of the interest she and Pascal had generated as they followed the maître d' to the table. While the establishment was much too exclusive for the clientele to seriously rubberneck, nevertheless their interest was undeniably piqued.

It was another strike against the man who sat opposite her now, broad and so handsome, that despite her antipathy she couldn't help that hot flutter of response.

He sat back in his chair. Alana could feel the whisper of his long legs stretching out under the table, and she tucked hers so tightly under her chair that it was uncomfortable.

'You don't have to worry, Alana, I'm under no illusions; you're compartmentalising this very much in the "work" box.'

She just looked at him, and he quirked a brow at her.

'The fact that you insisted on meeting me at my hotel

rather than let me pick you up from your home, the fact that you haven't changed out of your work clothes.'

Alana felt stiff and unbelievably vulnerable at the way he was so incisively summing her up. 'I didn't have time to change. And, yes, for me this is work.' She leaned forward slightly then. His perceptiveness made her feel cornered. 'I've had the experience of living with a level of public interest that I never want to invite into my life again. Being here with you, being seen with you, could put me in an awkward position. I don't want people to think we're here on some sort of date.' She sat back with her heart thumping at the way his face had darkened ominously.

'So who do you date, then, Alana?'

'I don't.'

'But you *were* married to Ryan O'Connor.'

The fact that he'd already found that out made her feel inordinately exposed. Her mouth twisted cynically. 'No doubt you didn't have to dig too deep to find that out.'

'No deeper than you dug to find out about my life.'

'That was for a professional interview.'

'Do I need to remind you that your questions didn't exactly follow the script?'

She flushed hotly. His eyes flashed with that same icy fire she'd witnessed earlier. She said defensively, 'You must know that if you open yourself up to any kind of press attention, then there's a risk that you'll be asked about things that are off-limits.'

He inclined his head, the ice still in his eyes. 'Of course; I'm not so naïve. But somehow I hadn't expected that of you.'

Ridiculously, Alana felt hurt and guilty. He was right; with another person who wasn't pushing her buttons so much, she would never have taken the initiative to ask unscripted questions. It had been her reaction to him that had prompted her to try and provoke a response that would take his intense interest off her, that playful teasing he'd seemed set to disarm her with. Again she wondered what she'd scratched the surface of earlier.

She opened her mouth, but at that moment a waitress arrived and distracted them by taking their orders. Conversation didn't resume until she had returned with a bottle of white wine. They'd both ordered fish. Once they were alone again, Pascal sat up straight. 'You can tell yourself that you're here for work, Alana, but I did not ask you here to talk about work. It's a subject I have to admit I find intensely boring when we could be discussing much more interesting things....'

'Such as?' she asked faintly, mesmerised by the way his eyes had changed again into warm pools of dark promise.

He took a sip of wine and she followed his lead unconsciously, her mouth feeling dry.

'Such as where you went last night, if you don't date.'

Initially Alana had felt herself automatically tensing up at his question, but then something happened. She found herself melting somewhere inside, and there was nothing she could do to stop it. Some part of her was responding to his heat, and it was just too hard not to give in just a little. So she told him about her brother's fortieth birthday. And that led to telling him about her six brothers and sisters. And her parents.

'They're *all* happily married with kids?'

Alana had to smile at the vague look of horror on his face. She knew people sometimes couldn't get over the entirely normal fact of large Irish families. She nodded, but felt that awfully familiar guilt strike her. She was the anomaly in her family. She tried to ignore the pain and spoke lightly. 'My family are a glowing testament to the institution. I have a grand total of fifteen nieces and nephews and my parents have been happily married for fifty years.'

He shook his head in disbelief. 'And where do you come?'

'I'm the baby. Ten years younger than my youngest

brother. Apparently I was a happy mistake. The age gap meant that despite coming from such a big family I've always felt in some ways like an only child. For most of the time that I can remember, it was just me and my parents.'

Alana fell silent as she thought of her parents. She was acutely aware of their increasing frailty, and especially her father, who had had a triple bypass the previous year. With her older siblings busy with families and their own problems, the care and concern of their parents largely fell to her. Not that she minded, of course. But she was aware nevertheless that they worried about her, that they wanted to see her settled like the others. Especially after Ryan.

Alana took a quick gulp of coffee and avoided Pascal's laser-like gaze. They'd finished their meal, and the plates had been cleared. It was as if he could see right through her head to her thoughts. She hoped the coffee would dilute the effect of the wine, which had been like liquid nectar. She'd shrugged off her jacket some time ago, and the silk of her shirt felt ridiculously sensual against her skin. And she found that it was all too easy to talk to Pascal Lévêque. He was attentive, charming, interested. *Interesting.*

But then he cut through her glow of growing warmth by asking softly, 'So what happened with you?'

At first she didn't understand. 'What do you mean?'

'Your marriage. You were about to divorce your husband when he died, weren't you?'

Immediately the glow left, Alana tensed. She could see his eyes flare, watching her retreat.

Unconsciously she felt for her jacket to pull it back on, instinctively seeking for some kind of armour. Her voice felt harsh. 'I see that whoever your source was didn't stop at the bare facts.'

Pascal's jaw clenched. 'I'm not judging you, Alana, or anything like it. I'm just asking a question. I can't imagine it was easy to take a decision to divorce, coming from the family that you've described.'

Her arms stilled in the struggle to get her jacket on; his perceptiveness sneaked into some very vulnerable part of her. He didn't know the half of it. Her own family still didn't know the half of it. They'd been as mystified and dismayed as the rest of the country at her behaviour. Something her husband had ruthlessly exploited in a bid to win as much sympathy as possible.

She broke eye contact with effort and finished the job of putting on her jacket. Finally she looked at him again. 'I'd really prefer not to talk about my marriage.'

Pascal was tempted to push her, but could see her clam up visibly. She'd become more and more relaxed over the course of the meal. He'd had to restrain his eyes from dropping numerous times to the soft swell of her breasts under the fine silk of her shirt. He still had no idea why she seemed so determined to cover up as much as possible. But, instead of his interest waning, the opposite was true. He had to admit that was part of the reason he'd asked her out—some kind of bid to have her reveal herself to be boring or diminish her attraction—yet she was intriguing him on levels that no other woman had ever touched.

He was not done with this, with her. But he knew that if he pushed her now, he could very well lose her. This was going to test all his patience and skill, but the chase was well and truly on. So now he flashed his most urbane smile and just said, 'No problem.' And he called for the bill. The abject relief on her face struck him somewhere powerful.

Pascal wouldn't listen to Alana's protests. He insisted on dropping her to her house, which was only ten minutes from the restaurant. Tucked in a small square in one of the oldest parts of Dublin, her house was a tiny cottage. Pascal's car was too big to navigate past all the parked cars at the opening of the square, and she jumped out. But he was quick, too, met her at the other side of the car and insisted on walking her up to her door.

She turned at the door, feeling absurdly threatened, but by something in herself more than him. Standing close together, her eye level was on his chest, and she looked up into his dark face. The moon gleamed brightly in a clear sky, and the February air was chill. But she didn't feel cold. She had the strongest feeling that if he attempted to kiss her, she wouldn't be able to stop him. And something within her melted at that thought. She blamed the wine. And his innate French seductiveness.

But then suddenly he moved back. Alana found herself making a telling movement towards him, as if attached by an invisible cord and she saw a flash of something in his eyes as if he, too, had noted and understood her movement.

Before she could clam up, he had taken her hand in his and was bending his head to kiss the back of it, exactly as he had the previous night in the hotel. His old-fashioned gesture touched and confused her. Her hormones were see-sawing with desires and conflicting tensions. And then, with a lingering, unfathomable look, he started to walk away down the small square and back to his car. Against every rational notion in her head, Alana found herself calling his name. He half-turned.

'I just…I just wanted to say thank you for dinner.'

He walked back up towards her with an intensity of movement that belied his easy departure just now. For a second she thought he was going to come right up to her and kiss her. She took a step back, feeling a mixture of panic and anticipation, with her heart thumping, but he stopped just short of her. He reached out a hand and tucked some hair behind her ear. It was a gesture he'd made earlier in the car, and she found herself wanting to turn her cheek into his palm. But then his hand was gone. And his eyes were glittering in the dark.

'You're welcome, Alana. But don't get too complacent. We will be meeting again, I can promise you that.'

He turned again and strode back to his car. He got in, shut the door and the car pulled away. And Alana just stood there, her mouth open. Heat flooded her body and something much worse—*relief*. She knew now that she had called his name and said thanks, because something about watching him walk away had affected her profoundly. She had an uncontrollable urge to stop him.

She had to face it—even though she'd been telling herself she wasn't interested in him from the moment their eyes had locked at the match, she *was*. He was smashing through the veritable wall she'd built around herself since she'd married Ryan O'Connor and her life had turned into a sort of living hell. It was frightening how, in the space of twenty-four hours, she found herself in a situation where she was actually feeling disappointed that a man she barely knew hadn't kissed her. Her famously cool poise, which hid all her bitter disappointments and broken dreams from everyone, even her own family, was suddenly very shaky.

By the time Alana was standing in her tiny galley-kitchen the next morning drinking her wake-up cup of tea, she felt much more in control. She only had to look around her house, in which she quite literally could not swing a cat, to feel on firmer ground. This was reality. This was all she'd been able to afford after Ryan had died. Her mouth tightened. Contrary to what everyone believed, she hadn't been left a millionairess after her football-star husband had died in the accident.

She was still picking up the pieces emotionally and financially from her five years of marriage. And, while her emotional scars might heal one day, the financial ones would be keeping her in this tiny cottage and working hard for a very long time. The truth was that Ryan had left astronomical debts behind him and, because their divorce hadn't come through by the time he'd died, they'd become Alana's responsibility. The sale of their huge house in the upmarket area of Dalkey had barely made a dent in what had been owed to various lenders.

Alana swallowed the last of her tea and grimaced as she washed out the cup. Pride was a terrible thing, she knew. But it had also given her a modicum of dignity. She'd never confided in anyone about the dire state of her marriage, had never told anyone about the day she'd walked into her bedroom to find Ryan in bed with three women who'd turned out to be call girls. They'd all been high on cocaine. He'd been too out of it to realise that it wasn't even his bedroom. By then, it had been at least three years since *they'd* shared a bed.

That had been the day that her humiliation had reached saturation point. The pressure of having to maintain a façade of a happy marriage had tipped over into unbearability. She'd left and filed for divorce.

But her wily husband had quickly made sure that it looked as though Alana had coldly kicked him out. She hadn't suspected his motives when he'd sheepishly offered to move out instead of her. But she should have known. The man she'd married had changed beyond all recognition as soon as he'd started earning enormous fees and tasted the heady heights of what it was to be a national superstar.

Admitting that she'd failed at her marriage had been soul destroying. She hadn't wanted to confide the awful reality of it to anyone. Even if she had wanted to, her father's health had been frail, and her mother had been focused solely on him. And, around the same time, one of her elder sisters had been diagnosed with breast cancer. With her sister having three children, and Alana being the only childless sibling and suddenly single again, she had moved into her sister's home to help her brother-in-law for the few months that Màire had spent getting treatment. Alana's marital problems had taken a backseat, and she'd been glad of the distraction while the divorce was worked out. She'd kept herself to herself and shunned her family's well-meaning probing, too heart-sore and humiliated even to talk about it.

It was exactly as Pascal had intuited last night, and she hated to admit that. It *had* been so hard, coming from a family of successfully married siblings, to be the only one to fail and to cause her parents such concern. Her monumental lack of judgement haunted her to this day. She obviously couldn't trust herself when it came to character assessment, never mind another man. And Pascal Lévêque was ringing so many bells that it should make it easy to reject his advances.

Alana brusquely pulled on her coat and got her keys. She refused to let her mind wander where it wanted: namely down a route that investigated the possibility of giving in to Pascal Lévêque's advances. Alana reassured herself that by now he'd have forgotten the wholly unremarkable Irish woman who had piqued his interest for thirty-six hours.

Thirty-six hours. That's all it had been. And yet it wasn't enough. Pascal stood at the window of his Paris office and looked out over the busy area of La Défense with its distinctive Grande Arche in the distance.

Alana Cusack was taking up a prominence in his head that was usually reserved for facts and figures. Ordinarily he could compartmentalise women very well; they didn't intrude on his every waking hour. They were for pleasure only, and fleeting pleasure at that. The minute he saw that look come into their eye, or heard that tone come into their voice, it was time to say goodbye. He enjoyed his freedom, the thrill of the chase, the conquest. No strings, no commitment.

But now a green-eyed, buttoned-up, starchy-collared, impertinent-questioning witch was making a hum of sexual frustration throb through his blood. He had to get her out of his system. Prove to himself that his desire had only been whetted because she was playing hard to get, and only because she *seemed* to be a little more intriguing than any other woman he'd met. The fact that she'd been married intrigued him too. Her marriage had obviously left her scarred. That had been clear from a mile away. Was that why she was so prickly, so uptight and defensive, so wary? Was she still grieving for her husband?

Pascal ran a hand through his hair impatiently. Enough! He turned his back on the view and called his PA into the room. She listened to his instructions and took down all the details, and she was professional enough not to give Pascal any indication that what he'd just asked her to do was in any way out of the ordinary.

But it was.

'There's something for you on your desk, Alana.'

'Thanks, Soph,' Alana answered distractedly as she flipped through her notes on her return from a lunchtime interview and walked into her tiny cubbyhole office just off the main newsroom. She looked up for a quick second to smile at Sophie, the general runaround girl, and her smile faltered when she saw the other girl's clearly mischievous look. With foreboding in her heart, Alana opened her door, and there on her desk was the biggest bunch of flowers she'd ever seen in her life. Her notebook and pen slid from her fingers onto the table. With a trembling hand, she plucked the card free from amongst the ridiculously extravagant blooms.

She cast a quick look back out the door, and seeing no one, quickly shut it. She ripped the envelope open and took out the card, which was of such luxurious quality that it felt about an inch thick between her fingers. All that was written on the card in beautiful calligraphy was one mystifying letter: 'I...'

She was completely and utterly bemused. Her dread was that they would be from him. But the card was enigmatic. They could actually be from anyone.

Not one person looked at her oddly afterwards, though, not even the junior reporter who covered current affairs who had drunkenly admitted at the office party last Christmas to having a crush on her. It wasn't her birthday, and she hadn't done an especially amazing babysitting-stint lately for any nieces or nephews, which sometimes resulted in flowers as a thank-you.

For the rest of the day Alana was like a cat on a hot tin roof. Distracted. She only left and brought the flowers home once she was sure nearly everyone had left the office.

The following day, as Alana walked in, flicking through her post, Sophie again said, 'Morning! There's something for you on your desk.'

Alana's heart stopped. It was like groundhog day. She went into her office with a palpitating heart and shut the door firmly behind her. Another bunch of flowers. Slightly different, but as extravagant as yesterday's. Her hands were sweating as she repeated the process of opening the envelope and taking out the card. This one read: 'will...'

By the end of the week Alana sat at the wooden table in her sitting room and felt a little numb. The smell of flowers was overpowering in the tiny artisan-cottage. A vase sat in the centre of the table abundant with blooms. And also on the table in front of her, neatly lined up in a row, were the five cards that had accompanied a different bunch of flowers every single day of the week.

All together, they now made sense: 'I will see you tonight'.

But of course she'd known what the full meaning of the

cards was when she'd received the fifth one that morning. All day she'd experienced a fizzing in her veins and a sick churning in her belly. She'd vaguely thought of going to the cinema, or seeing if friends wanted to go out, anything to avoid being at home where she was sure he was going to call. An awful sense of inevitability washed over her. She wasn't ready for this. She would just have to make him see that and send him on his way. But still…the gesture, the flowers, and his obvious intention to fly all the way back to Dublin just to see her, was nothing short of overwhelming.

Her phone rang shrilly in the silence and she jumped violently, her heart immediately hammering. Her mouth was dry. 'Hello?'

'What's this about you and Pascal Lévêque?'

Alana sagged onto the arm of her sofa. 'Ailish.' Her oldest and bossiest sister was always guaranteed to raise her hackles. Twenty years separated them, and sometimes Ailish came across as a little overbearing to say the least. She meant well, though, which took the sting out of her harsh manner.

'So? What's going on? Apparently one of the world's most eligible bachelors took you out for dinner last weekend.'

Tension held Alana's body straight. 'How did you hear about it?'

'It was in the tabloids today.'

Alana groaned inwardly, wondering how she'd missed that. Someone at work must have leaked the story. God knew, enough people had heard him ask her. And it wouldn't have taken a rocket scientist to work out who the flowers had been from, either.

'Look, I interviewed him and he took me for dinner, that's all. Nothing is going on.' The betraying vision of her house full to the roof with flowers made her wince.

Her sister harumphed down the phone. 'Well, I just hope you're not going to be gracing the tabloids every day with tales of sexual exploits with a Casanova like that. I mean, can you imagine if Mam and Dad saw that? It was bad enough having to defend you to practically the whole nation after you threw Ryan out—'

Alana stood up, her whole body quivering. The memory of her parents' lined and worried faces was vivid. And her guilt. 'Ailish, what I do and who I see is none of your business. Do I comment on your marriage to Tom?'

'You wouldn't need to,' replied her sister waspishly. 'We're not the ones being discussed over morning coffee by the nation.'

Alana heard her doorbell ring and she automatically went to answer it. 'Like I said, what I do is none of your business.' Her sister's 'judge and jury' act made anger throb through her veins, and she knew her voice was rising. She struggled for a minute with the habitually stiff lock, and tucked the phone between her neck and shoulder to use both hands.

'I am a fully grown woman and I can see who I want, go where I want, and have sex with who I want whenever I please.'

The door finally opened. Her words hung on the cool evening air as she took in the devastatingly gorgeous sight of Pascal Lévêque just standing there, turning her inner-city enclave into something much more exotic. Her heart-rate soared. She'd forgotten all about him in the space of the last few seconds, and the high emotion her sister had been evoking. In her shock she lifted her head and her phone dropped to the ground with a tinny clatter.

Pascal swiftly bent and picked it up.

An irate voice could be heard: 'Alana? *Alana!*'

Alana couldn't take her eyes off Pascal. She took her phone back, lifted it to her ear and said vaguely, 'Ailish, someone's just arrived. I'll call you back, OK?'

Words resounded in her head: *too late to escape now.*

# CHAPTER THREE

By the time Alana had stepped back into her house, followed by a tall, dark and imposing Pascal Lévêque, the shock was rapidly wearing off. She crossed her arms and rounded on him with a scowl on her face. Once again he was demonstrating that ability to suck in the space around him and make everything seem more intense—dwarfed. She tried to block out the fact that he was quite simply the most handsome man who'd ever stood feet away from her and looked at her with an intensity that bordered on being indecent.

'That phone call was a conversation that shouldn't have had to happen. And it was all your fault.'

He inclined his head slightly. He looked *huge* in her tiny sitting room. 'I apologise, but, as all I heard was the intriguing last sentence, you'll have to forgive me as I don't know what I've done. And *we* certainly haven't had sex yet.'

Alana flushed when she recalled what she'd been saying to her sister as she'd opened the door. 'Did you know that apparently our dinner date was in the papers today?' Defensive, angry energy radiated off her in waves. She could almost see them, like a heat haze.

He shook his head, his eyes never leaving hers, hypnotising her. 'No. I wasn't aware of that. But of course, there were people at the restaurant, and I would imagine that one or two people heard me ask you at the studio; perhaps it was leaked.'

Alana laughed out loud. 'One or two? Try the whole crew standing in the room. It's recorded on tape, for God's sake.'

He started to shrug off his big, black overcoat and proceeded to whip out a bottle of wine from somewhere, like a magician. Panic flowed through Alana. She put out her hands as if that might halt him. 'What do you think you're doing? Stop taking off your coat right now.'

She shook her head emphatically. 'No way; you are not coming in here with a bottle of wine, and we are not going to be having a cosy chat.'

For a big man he moved swiftly and gracefully. His coat was already draped over one arm, the bottle of red wine in one hand, long fingers visible. She remembered him holding her hands, entwining those fingers with hers. A pulse throbbed between her legs.

She looked up at him and knew she must look slightly desperate—she felt desperate.

'I don't mind where we go, Alana, but I've come all this way to see you, so you're not getting away.'

His voice was like deep velvet over steel. He meant what he said.

She gulped. 'What do you want?' she asked weakly. He was threatening and invading every aspect of what had been up till now her impregnable defence.

Pascal restrained himself from telling her exactly what he wanted. He didn't want to frighten her off. But what he wanted very much involved a lot less clothes and a flat, preferably soft surface. She was dressed all in black, her hair tied back. Not a stiff shirt this time, but a roll-neck top that effectively concealed everything. And yet the material had to be cashmere or something, because it clung to her torso and chest, and for the first time he could see the proper shape of her. The thrust of her breasts against the fabric was sensual torture. They were perfectly formed, high and firm. He could imagine that they would fill his hands like ripe, succulent fruits, their tips hardening against the palm of his hand... He slammed the door on his rampant imaginings. His arousal was springing to life. He forced himself to sound reasonable, calm.

'What I would like is to share this bottle of wine with you and to talk. We can go somewhere else if you'd prefer.'

Alana looked at him suspiciously, hating this invasion of her space. He was as immoveable as a rock. If they went somewhere else that would involve more time. If they stayed here, he'd be gone sooner. She made her reluctant decision and reached out a hand.

'We might as well stay here. It's a Friday night; most places in town would be like cattle markets by now.'

Despite her obvious lack of delight at the prospect, Pascal carefully masked the intense surge of triumph he felt and handed over the wine, even being careful to make sure their hands didn't touch, knowing that could set him back. *Dieu!* This woman was like an assault on his every sense. He hadn't imagined her allure, she was more vivid, more sexy, more *everything*, in the flesh.

As Alana went into the galley-kitchen, she was aware of him moving into the sitting room, hands in the pockets of his trousers and looking around. She sent him a surreptitious glance. He was dressed smartly—dark trousers and a light shirt, top button open as if he'd discarded a tie somewhere. He must have come straight from work—on a private plane? Somehow she couldn't imagine him queueing up with lesser mortals for a scheduled flight. He was the kind of man who would stride across the tarmac and climb into a sleek, snazzy jet.

'You got my flowers, I see.'

Alana's hand stilled on the bottle opener for a moment. She looked at him. 'Yes, thank you.' She cringed inwardly. Had he seen the cards all laid out in a row on the table as he'd come in? 'You shouldn't have, though. It caused no amount of speculation at work, and I'd really prefer if you didn't.' God, she sounded so uptight. And what was to say he'd ever send her flowers again anyway?

'As you can see, this house isn't exactly big enough to take them.'

Pascal looked around and thought privately that this was hardly what she must have been used to, as Ryan O'Connor's wife. It made her even more enigmatic. She was fast proving that, whatever scene she'd been a part of in the past, that was not who she was now. 'No, I guess not. I'm sorry if I embarrassed you, Alana, I merely wanted to show you that I meant what I said, about seeing you again, and I didn't have your number, so...'

Alana stabbed the cork with the bottle opener. 'It's fine; forget it. The old-folks' home around the corner were delighted, as they got the other half of the flower shop you sent.'

She sent him a small, rueful smile then, unable to help herself. She didn't like being ungrateful for gifts.

Pascal was looking at her with an arrested expression on his face, his eyes intent on the area of her mouth. Her lips tingled. Alana's hands stopped on the cork. 'What is it?'

But then his eyes lifted to hers as if she'd imagined it, and he went back to looking at her books and prints. 'Nothing.'

Eventually she pulled the cork free with a loud pop and got down two glasses from her open shelves. She poured the wine and handed him a glass, keeping one for herself.

He stood looking at her for a long moment and then held his glass out. Her heart thumped at what he might say, but all he said was, *'Santé.'*

She clinked her glass to his and replied with the Irish, '*Sláinte*.'

They both took a sip. She couldn't quite believe that he was standing here in front of her. The wine was like liquid velvet, fragrant, round and smooth. Clearly very expensive. Alana indicated for him to sit on her couch. He did, and dwarfed the three-seater. She sat in the armchair opposite. The lighting was soft and low. The space far too intimate. This was her sanctuary, her place of refuge. And yet, having him here wasn't generating the effect that she would have expected. She was still angry, yes—but more than that was something else, something like excitement.

She thought of something then as her stomach growled quietly. 'Have you eaten?'

He took another drink from his glass and shook his head. 'No.' He just realised then that he'd hardly eaten all day; he'd been so consumed with getting out of Paris and over here. It made him feel uncomfortable now.

Alana put down her glass and stood up. 'I was going to make myself something to eat…that is, if you want something, too?'

'That would be great, I'm starving.' He smiled, and the room seemed to tilt for a second.

Alana picked up her glass and backed into the kitchen, which was just feet away from where he now sat with an arm stretched out over the back of the sofa. At home, as if he dropped in all the time from Paris. She couldn't think of that now.

'It's just fish, lemon sole, nothing too exciting. But I have two…'

He nodded. 'That sounds perfect. Thank you.'

Alana busied herself turning on the oven and putting potatoes on to boil. When she looked back over to the sitting room, she could see that Pascal was looking through her CDs.

She had a moment of clarity. What was she doing? She was meant to be rushing him out of the house, not cooking him dinner! But, she had to concede, it had been easy to ask him. And he *had* sent her all those amazing flowers. If she was never going to see him after tonight, then what was the harm in a little dinner?

Happy that she'd justified her actions to herself, and not willing to pay attention to the hum of *something* in her blood, when she heard the strains of her favourite jazz CD coming from the sound system, she found it soothing rather than scary.

'I hope you don't mind?'

She looked over to where Pascal was hunched down at the system, the material of his trousers and shirt straining over taut, hard muscles in his thighs and back. She shook her head, her mouth feeling very dry.

'No…no.' She took another hasty gulp of wine. *Oh God.*

By the time Alana was taking his cleared plate from him, and apologising again that their dinner had been on their knees, she was smiling at something he'd just said. As she'd been preparing the dinner, they'd started up an innocuous conversation, and in the course of eating had managed to touch on films, books, French politics, the Six Nations and rugby. She'd found herself telling him about her father's career playing for Ireland, unable to keep the pride from her voice. And she hadn't mistaken the gleam of something unfathomable in his eyes. Even though he'd told her he hadn't wanted to play, had he harboured ambitions?

She came back and sat down, tucking her legs under her. She'd slipped off her shoes. She felt energised, zingy, as if she could stay up all night.

To her surprise, she saw Pascal look at his watch and then he drained his glass of wine. He stood up and Alana felt unaccountably disorientated. She stood too. The space between them was electric.

'I'm afraid I have to go.'

Alana immediately felt crushed, silly, exposed. She should have been grinning from ear to ear, racing to hand him his coat, saying good riddance—so why did she feel her stomach hollowing out at the thought? The old pain of past misjudgements rose up like a spectre.

'Oh, well. I can imagine you must have some business here. Somewhere else to be?'

He shook his head and came close. Alana couldn't back away as the chair was just behind her legs. Her heart was thumping so hard she felt it must be visible under her top.

'I've got important meetings at home all weekend. It's too boring to go into. But I need to make my flight slot tonight, otherwise I'll miss my first meeting in the morning.'

Alana's jaw dropped. 'You're going back to *Paris*? Now?' He nodded.

The knowledge was having trouble sinking into her brain: he had come all the way to Dublin just to see her for a few hours; it was too much for her to take in.

'I…I…'

Her shock was obviously transparent.

He pulled a quirky, sexy smile. 'It was worth it, Alana. Just to see you again. I've been thinking about you all week. I can't seem to get you out of my head.'

'I…' Her powers of speech had been rendered null and void. He was coming closer, making speech even more elusive and unlikely.

He was now so close that her head was tipped back to look into those dark, dark eyes. She felt a warm finger come under her chin, stroking the smooth skin, his thumb on her chin. She couldn't move.

His scent enveloped her in a haze of desire, desire that

she'd never felt before. She fancied that she could hear his heartbeat too. Then he spoke and his voice was harsh. 'I told myself I wouldn't do this now. But…I can't *not*. You're more intoxicating to me than anything or anyone I've ever known. And all week I've been imagining what it would be like.'

She swallowed, 'What *what* would be like?' But she knew. And heaven help her but she'd been imagining it too. She knew she had; she'd just been denying it.

He said the words and something awful like relief flowed through her.

'To kiss you.'

With his finger still under her chin, no other parts of their bodies touching, he bent his head to hers. Past, present and future collided in the moment that her eyelids fluttered closed, and she felt his mouth touch hers. It was a brief press of his lips to hers, a testing, tasting. But it ignited a flame of raw desire along every one of Alana's veins.

When he drew back slightly, she made a treacherous sound in her throat. She wanted more than that brief all-too-chaste kiss. And so did he evidently.

This time it wasn't chaste and benedictory, this time it was forceful, both their mouths pressing together, tasting, experiencing. The finger at her chin was gone. His hand slid round to the back of her head, flicked away the band tying her hair in a ponytail and threaded through the soft, silky strands to cradle her skull in his hand. His other arm slid around her slim waist and pulled her into him. Her arms automatically went to his shoulders and clung for support.

The feel of his body pressed up close to hers was short-circuiting her system. He was hard all over, and so strong. She could feel his chest muscles flex against her soft curves when his arm tightened around her, pulling her even closer.

While their bodies melded together, their mouths remained fused. Pascal pulled back briefly and Alana looked up into those amazing eyes that were burning, reflecting a fire she felt deep in her belly, where a very hard part of him was making her want to move restlessly. She was stunned by everything. She felt confused; she could feel herself tremble with reaction. She frowned slightly, her mouth opened.

Pascal pressed a finger to her mouth. The softness of her lips and her warm breath made him harder, and he almost groaned out loud with the need to take her now, to sink into her yielding, silky warmth. But he knew that she wasn't far from letting her head take over, from possibly pushing him away. 'Don't think. Don't speak. Just *feel*.'

This time when his mouth touched hers it was slightly open. Breaths mingled and wove together, and for one split second neither of them breathed. And then Pascal slid his tongue between her lips and Alana's hands clutched at his shoulders. She'd been kissed like this before; of course she had. But whenever Ryan had kissed her, it had always been rough and with no finesse.

But this was in another league. Pascal's tongue danced erotically with hers, advanced and retreated, inviting her to follow him. And she did. Winding her arms tight around his neck, pressing even closer, she slid her tongue into his mouth and was rewarded with a low guttural moan. It was the sexiest feeling, and she was controlling the pace, the movements. She savoured his full lower lip, felt it with her tongue, let it glide across the surface before allowing their tongues to duel again.

When she felt him snake a hand under her top, to feel the skin above her trousers, the curve of her waist, her legs trembled in earnest. Their kisses stilled for a second, as if he was waiting to see what signal she would give. She nipped his lower lip gently and she could feel him half-smile against her mouth.

His hand slid higher over her smooth back, to just below the clasp of her bra. His hand was so big she imagined it could span her entire back. With a practised flick of his wrist and fingers, he opened the clasp. Alana felt her bra loosen, but she was lost in a maelstrom of lust so strong that she wanted nothing more than for him take the weight and fullness of her breast into his palm—which he promptly did, sliding his whole hand around her ribs as if loath not to caress every part of her. The sensation was so shockingly electric that she gasped and wrenched her mouth from his, breathing jerkily.

His other hand still cradled her head; their bodies were still fused at every conceivable point. She was on her tiptoes to try and keep his hardness there, at the apex of her thighs where a loud, heavy beat of blood called to her. She couldn't do anything but look up into his glittering, aroused gaze as his hand cupped her heavy flesh and his thumb moved back and forth over the tingling, tight peak of her nipple.

She bit her lip, and he bent his head to whisper hotly in her ear, 'I want to take it into my mouth until you come apart in my arms…until you're so wet that sliding into you will be the easiest thing in the world.'

A million things were hurtling into Alana's head. Past experiences, warnings, wants and confusion reigned. What was happening to her? She should be shocked, but she wasn't. She'd never thought in a million years she could respond like this, and yet they had done little more here and now than she'd already experienced at teen discos years ago. Or during her marriage.

Pascal could see the way her eyes were clearing, the way those green depths were starting to swirl. He had to pull back, even if it was going to kill him. Gently he closed her bra again and stepped back slightly to pull down her top. He'd been right; her body with its gentle curves was infinitely more alluring than he'd ever expected it to be, her breasts fuller. It was a crime that she hid under those structured tops and dark colours.

He put his hands on her shoulders and stepped back completely, and tried to ignore the inferno raging in his pants.

'I have to go. I wish I didn't, but I do. You could come with me?' he asked then, but already he could see her start to tense, stiffen.

'No,' he answered for her. 'It's too soon.' He castigated himself for his lack of control.

He walked over to get his coat which was draped on the back of a chair, and pulled it on. He saw the cards that had accompanied the flowers neatly lined up to show the sentence they'd spelt out. Something forceful struck him then. He'd never gone to such trouble before. Women always said yes; it was always easy. But recently his experiences with women had always proved somewhat unsatisfactory. And now merely kissing Alana was making him feel like a randy teenager again.

Alana welcomed the distance as she watched him put his coat on, accentuating his shoulders, his broad back. His shoulders that she'd just been clutching with complete abandon, because if she hadn't, she'd have dissolved at his feet. What had he done to her? What the hell did he think he was doing, waltzing in here for just a few hours only to mess up her carefully controlled world? She crossed her arms over still tight and sensitive breasts.

He turned around and saw her look immediately. 'Don't look at me like that.'

Alana's jaw tensed so hard she felt it might break. 'I don't want this. I don't want you.'

He covered the paltry distance between them in a couple of steps, floorboards creaking under his weight.

'I think I've just proven that you *do* want me. And I want you. Badly.'

In a shocking move he took her hand and brought it down to where she could feel his agony for herself. Hectic colour flooded her cheeks.

'There's something rare and powerful between us, Alana, and I won't let you shut me out just because you're scared.'

She snatched her hand back from where the hard evidence of his arousal was threatening to overheat her brain again. 'I am *not* scared.' *Liar.* 'I just don't want this. I really don't want this.'

His stance was strong, legs planted wide, face implacable. 'It's already happening. We can't go back now. You could have sent back the flowers, or thrown them out.' He flung out a hand. 'But you didn't. You could have refused to let me come into your house tonight, but you didn't.'

Humiliation coursed through her. He was right. She'd put up absolutely no fight whatsoever. What was she doing? Had she learnt nothing?

'You're covering the match in Italy next weekend in Stadio Flaminio?'

His abrupt change of subject caught her unawares. 'Yes. Yes, I am.'

'I have an apartment in Rome. Come over on Friday night and stay with me for the weekend. I have to go to the match, too, and my bank is sponsoring a charity ball on Saturday night—you could come with me.'

Alana automatically shook her head and quailed slightly under the harsh light in his eyes.

'My flight on Saturday morning is booked already. I'm going with colleagues. And I'm due back on Sunday morning. It's all organised.'

'And do you always do what you're told?' he asked softly, softly enough to disarm her for a second. It made a poignant memory rise up. She hadn't always been so conventional, so careful to stick to the rules. There had been a time when she'd been very much a free spirit. That was how she'd met Ryan; she'd fallen for the passionate free spirit she'd seen in him. But she'd had it all wrong. His passion had never been for her or even life. It had been for money, fame and adulation. And then he'd slowly killed any such impulse in her, reducing her to a shadow of her former self.

Alana looked up. Caught between two worlds and painful memories, she found herself instinctively clinging on to something in Pascal's eyes.

'I will have my plane at your disposal.'

'But that's crazy.'

He shushed her. 'At your disposal. It will be at Dublin airport on Friday evening, ready to take you to Rome to meet me. I would like you to use it, Alana. I would like you to stay with me. I won't force you into anything you're not comfortable with. Or ready for.'

She would have laughed, but the intensity in his face stopped her. He was holding out a card. She took it warily.

'Those are all my numbers, and my assistant's numbers. If you're going to come on Friday, just call her and give her your passport details and she'll give you all the information and arrange for a pick-up to deliver you to the plane.'

*To deliver her to him like a gift-wrapped parcel.*

Everything in Alana rebelled at the thought of being so easy, so compliant. But another part of her was beating hard at the thought of how easy it would be to just...do this. Had she really envisaged living her entire life celibate? While she knew well that Pascal took women for just a finite amount of time, perhaps that was what she needed—a no-strings affair. He was already smashing the awful, soul-destroying belief that somehow she'd been frigid. But then, if Pascal discovered the extent of her lack of experience, would he be turned off? Doubts crowded her mind again. How could she even be seriously contemplating this?

And now he really was leaving, opening the small hall door, ducking his head to go out through the front door.

She forced her stricken limbs to move, and followed him.

When he turned round, she was on her step. Before she could move, he'd pulled her into him and pressed his mouth to hers, sliding his tongue between her lips, making her heart beat fast and her blood turn to treacle in seconds. She could already feel herself melting. And then he pulled away and set her back.

'See?' was all he said, was all he had to say. He backed away and then turned to walk down the square. As if by magic a sleek, dark car pulled up at the bottom of the square and then he was getting into the back and was gone. Alana's hands curled into fists at her sides, her emotions and hormones in chaotic turmoil. Every carefully erected piece of defence was crashing and burning. There was no way she would take him up on his offer. No way.

Those very words came back to mock Alana as she sat in the back of a very familiar, luxurious Lexus which was speeding through the usual tangled Dublin Friday-night rush hour like a hot knife through butter, almost as if Pascal had decreed it. Not even the traffic was giving her a chance to stop and think, to change her mind. Her small weekend-bag was in the boot. And she couldn't even reassure herself that it had been a last-minute decision; she'd packed her bag last night as if on autopilot, as if somehow it hadn't really been her doing it.

And then she'd brought it to work that morning, and had coolly informed her boss that she'd made alternative arrangements for getting to Rome. And then she'd rung Pascal's assistant, and told her that she'd be on the plane that evening. His assistant had been brisk and efficient, ringing back within ten minutes with the details of who would be picking her up, leaving her no time to think about backing out.

And now here she was.

On the way to becoming Pascal Lévêque's newest lover.

And her only reaction was one of intense anticipation. She'd finally had to give into it. She'd vacillated each torturous day that week, from vowing absolutely that she would do no such thing, to staring into space, remembering what it had been like to have him kiss her, and wanting him with a hunger that shocked her.

He'd called to speak to her every evening, too, having made sure to take her number, but had never mentioned Rome. He'd ask her about her day, and tell her a little about his. He was a master tactician, slowly but surely wearing down her defences. She'd found herself looking forward to speaking to him. It was when she'd woken in the middle of the previous night, to find herself in tangled sheets damp with sweat after an intensely erotic dream, that she'd got up and packed. It was only after she'd done that, she'd been able to go back to sleep.

Another dark, sleek car with tinted windows was waiting on the tarmac at the airport in Rome. She'd seen it out of the window as they'd landed. Now she took a deep breath, her case in a white-knuckle grip as the air steward waited for the door to open. Alana straightened her short jacket over her dress. She hadn't changed from her work clothes, her *armour*. A black pinafore dress, complete with shirt and tie, stockings and high-heeled shoes.

The clunking noise of the steps being wheeled to the aircraft made her jump, and she smiled nervously at the steward, wondering in a fleeting, scary moment how many women he'd escorted to meet Pascal like this. All of a sudden she wanted to go, leave. She'd made a huge mistake.

But then the door opened and there was nowhere to go but forward.

And there he was. It was too late to turn back now.

It was dark and slightly chilly as she walked down the steps. Pascal was waiting at the bottom, dressed casually in jeans, looking relaxed, vibrant and beautiful. He didn't move to touch her, and he didn't look triumphant. And she was grateful, because if he had she might have scuttled back up the steps and ordered the pilot to take her back home.

'Here, let me.' He took her case and the driver transferred it to the boot of the car. Pascal indicated for her to get in. And then he shut the door and walked round to the other side. The door closed and they were moving.

Enclosed in the intimate space, Alana felt as if she were on fire. Suddenly her shirt and tie were ridiculously restrictive. She couldn't look at Pascal. Silence thickened, but it wasn't awkward. As they approached the city, Pascal started pointing out landmarks in a neutral, deep voice. Just that alone had an effect on her body, the fine hairs standing up all over her skin. Yet it was also calming, as if he were trying to soothe her. She still hadn't looked directly at him, but then she felt his hand, warm and very real on her chin and jaw, turning her head towards him.

Did she have any idea how beautiful she looked? Did she have any idea what her effect on him was in those clothes? That damn shirt and tie had featured in every fantasy that had kept him awake, tossing and turning, all week. Her eyes were huge, staring at him with a mixture of fear and trepidation.

'Thank you,' he said huskily.

She swallowed, and he could feel the small movement. He couldn't take his hand from her chin. He wanted to smooth and caress the silky skin all over her body.

'I'm still...not sure that I'm doing the right thing.' She looked for a second as if she were gearing herself up for something, and then she said in a rush, 'How many women have you had delivered to you by plane like that?'

Her honesty hit him between the eyes. He knew this was important. This could determine the weekend—*them*. He didn't have to lie. 'No one. I have travelled on that plane with women, but I've never sent it especially for someone before.

Alana, you wouldn't be here if you didn't think this was right. Don't you trust your own judgement?'

The minute he'd said the words he could feel her tense, could see her withdraw mentally and physically. What had he said?

She reached up and took his hand down. 'That's just the problem,' she said with a sterile voice. 'My track record when it comes to judgement leaves a lot to be desired.'

Her husband—she had to be referring to her marriage. It made him want to quiz her, ask her what she meant. But he wasn't in the habit of wanting to know extraneous personal details of his lovers' past experiences, and he rejected the desire now. Pascal wanted her attention back with him with an urgency that bordered on the painful. He found her hand and wound his fingers through hers, not letting her pull away.

'Alana, this thing between us is too important to ignore. Trust *that*, if nothing else.'

She knew that it would have been the height of naïvety to assume that Pascal had never taken another lover on his plane. She gave up trying to pull her hand away and let it rest in his. She also gave up trying to avoid his eyes. They glowed with dark embers of sensual promise.

A hum of electricity flowed between them. He wasn't exaggerating; she'd never ever thought anyone would make her feel this way. She'd once foolishly and romantically thought that this was the way she'd feel with her husband.

But she hadn't.

And she'd blamed herself for that—but for the first time she could see more clearly that it had been just as much Ryan's fault as her own.

Perhaps this was her chance to start living again, to stop closing herself off to the world in some kind of misplaced penance she felt she owed. Her husband had taken enough of her life and soul. It was time to take some back for herself.

'We're here.'

Alana's hand tightened reflexively in Pascal's. He didn't rush her. He let her take a look outside the car. They were on a quiet street. Old stone steps led up to a foliage-covered walkway through which Alana could see a massive, ornate door.

When the driver had taken out her case and walked round to open her door, Pascal finally released her hand and she got out. The Rome night air was cool and fragrant. Pascal picked up her case and took her hand, leading her up the garden path; she wasn't unaware of the metaphor. He let go of her to open the door. All was darkness when they walked in at first, but then Pascal flicked a switch nearby and lights came on, low and intimate. Alana gasped. It was stunning.

A huge, lofty high-ceilinged room with massive windows led in one direction into a large kitchen, and the other direction into a huge open-plan living area. It was all decorated in white, prints on the walls and dramatic cushions on the couches adding splashes of colour. Inexplicably, this heartened Alana. She wasn't sure what she had been expecting, but she knew that if Pascal had shown her into some kind of sterile bachelor-pad all her misgivings would have returned with a vengeance.

'Come; I'll show you upstairs.'

Wordlessly, she followed him up a wide staircase to the side of the living area. Upstairs were huge windows. He showed her into a big bedroom. The feel of deep, luxurious carpet underfoot made her instinctively bend to take off her shoes. She saw him look and grimaced slightly, holding her shoes in her hands. 'I hope you don't mind. My feet are killing me.'

He shook his head. 'Not at all.' He put her case down at the bottom of the king-sized bed that was dressed in Egyptian cotton. 'This is your room, Alana.'

He walked to the door and gestured across the hall to where she could see in through an open door to another dimly lit large room, dressed in more masculine tones. 'That's my room.' He turned then and stuck his hands in his pockets. 'Obviously I would prefer you to share my room with me, but it'll be your move to make.'

Alana bit her lip. He couldn't know how important it was to her that he wasn't pushing her. 'Thank you. I appreciate that.'

He held out a hand. 'Leave your things there. You must be hungry; I'll prepare us something to eat downstairs.'

Alana shrugged off her jacket to lay it over the back of a chair, and felt the energy zip up her arm when she took his hand.

'You can cook?' she asked a little breathlessly as he led her out in her stockinged feet.

He glanced back with a smile. 'I can just about manage to burn some pasta and tomato sauce. Are you hungry?'

Just then her stomach rumbled. She smiled too. 'Starving.'

With a full stomach and a languorous feeling snaking through her bones, Alana walked around the downstairs living-area with a glass of wine in her hand, looking at Pascal's prints and sculptures. She was transfixed by one photograph; something about it was very familiar. It was black and white, an old man's face, gnarled and lined, very dark, even a hint of some other exotic lineage. His eyes were remarkable, deep set and black, holding such a wealth of emotion that Alana could feel it reach out and envelop her. There was everything in that expression: regret, pain, love, passion, disappointment, hope.

'That's my grandfather.'

She turned round. Pascal was a few feet behind her, looking at the photograph. She could see the resemblance now, except Pascal's eyes were unreadable.

'Did you take it?'

He shook his head. In an instant Pascal knew instinctively that Alana had seen the same things he saw whenever he looked at the picture. No one else had ever stood transfixed by it before. It made something feel weak in his chest. He avoided her eye, his voice gruff. 'No; my talents lie solely in facts and figures. This was taken by an American photographer who was travelling around the south of France. After my grandfather died, I tracked him down and got a print.'

'You must have been very close; you mentioned that you spent time with him.'

Pascal just nodded. She didn't probe any more. She understood the need to keep things back. She knew he was watching her as she continued to walk around, taking sips of wine, feeling the surface of a smooth Roman bust beneath her fingers.

Every one of Pascal's senses was pulled as taut as a bow string as he watched her hand smooth over the head of the bust, wanting her hand to be smoothing over him. He had to wonder if perhaps her air of vulnerability, her apparent lack of experience, was all an act, designed to entice, tease, seduce. She'd let her hair down, and it was slightly tousled from where she'd run her hands through it, but it wasn't tousled enough for him yet.

She turned then, and he could see that her glass of wine was empty. He made as if to get the bottle and top her up, but she shook her head jerkily. She was going to make him wait; he knew it. She wasn't ready. His desire, already at boiling point, would have to settle to a simmer for now.

Alana had turned with every intention of asking for some more wine, but she could already feel the effects. Desire hung between them, heavy and potent. *Too much too soon.* Pascal stood just feet away, but when he moved as if to give her some more she shook her head. She couldn't do this now. She wasn't ready, and she could see that he'd already read that in

her expression before she'd known it herself. That discon-
certed her. She wasn't used to people intuiting her intentions.

'You must be tired.'

She forced a smile. She was anything but. 'I was up early.
Would you mind if I went to bed?' *'Alone'* hung between
them along with the desire, but it seemed to make it even
heavier, denser. Was she doing the right thing? Her body told
her no, her head said yes.

He shook his head, jaw rigid, eyes black. 'Of course not.
What time do you have to be in work tomorrow?'

Such banalities.

Alana glanced at her watch, but didn't even register the
time. 'I have to meet the crew in Stadio Flaminio at midday;
the kick-off is at 3:00 p.m.'

He nodded. 'My car will take you in and come back for
me.'

'If you're sure? I could get a taxi.'

He shook his head almost violently, and Alana knew the
sudden urge to leave, get away now. It was as if his control
was barely leashed.

He took the glass from her hand. *'Dors bien*, Alana.'

# CHAPTER FOUR

WHEN Alana reached her room, she was breathing hard. She went straight into her *en suite* bathroom and looked in the mirror. Her cheeks were flushed, eyes over-bright. Her body was too sensitive, and an ache throbbed down low in her belly and between her legs. She dropped her head, hands gripping the edge of the sink.

She went back out into the bedroom and fooled herself into believing that she was doing what she wanted by unpacking her clothes and taking out her toiletries. A silk dress slithered out of her trembling hands to the ground. She picked it up. She'd pulled it out of her wardrobe on a whim. It was one of the very few dresses she'd kept from her days with Ryan, and she hadn't worn it since her marriage had ended. Ryan had derided her when she'd worn it first, as it hadn't been revealing enough for him...or, more accurately, for the press, who he'd constantly wanted to impress. But in actual fact it was plenty revealing, and way more than Alana had been comfortable with. *Up to now.*

She hung it up abruptly, refusing to think about why she'd brought it.

As she was about to start undressing, she stopped and sat on the edge of the bed. Her heart was thumping slow, heavy beats. She was shaking. Adrenaline washed through her system. Her body already knew what was inevitable. She couldn't deny it to herself. It was as if the centre of her being had become magnetised and could only go in one direction.

She walked back over to the door and opened it. The only light came from downstairs. She paused at the top of the stairs. He was still down there, sitting on the couch, long legs splayed in front of him, in bare feet, the dregs of a glass of wine in his hands into which he was staring broodily. Fear assailed Alana again, and she almost fled, but then he looked up.

Tension snaked up from him to her and an unspoken plea: *don't go*. She realised that she couldn't, even if she'd wanted to. She came down the stairs, clinging onto the rail as she went. She was melting inside as she came closer and closer. Her clothes felt restrictive.

She got to the bottom. Without taking his eyes off hers, he carefully placed his glass on the small table at his feet and stood up. She concentrated on his eyes—dark, molten.

'I couldn't sleep.'

He didn't smile, but she heard the smile in his voice. 'You were only gone ten minutes.'

'I know I won't be able to sleep.'

'What do you want, Alana?'

She shook her head. 'I want…I want…' Her face flamed. 'You know what I want. Don't make me say it, please.'

'Show me what you want.' His voice was soft, silky, heavy with erotic promise.

He was making her come to him all the way. Making sure.

Alana stepped forward jerkily until she was standing right in front of him. She could barely breathe. They hardly touched, and now she lifted her hands to his shoulders. They were so much wider and higher than she remembered. She took another couple of awkward steps. He was making no move to help her.

She looked up at him, a hint of desperation on her face; she could feel sweat on her brow. 'Can't you just…?'

'You want me to take you? To take the decision out of your hands—so on some level you don't have to actually make it clear what you want?' He shook his head. 'No. I need to know that you really want this. I won't indulge regrets and recriminations in the morning.'

Damn him. Since when had he become a psychoanalyst? But Alana's need was too great.

She moved even closer and wound her arms around his neck, bringing her whole body flush against his, leaning into him. Her breasts were crushed into his chest, and she felt him suck in a deep breath. It made her exultant. He might be displaying control, but she guessed it was shaky.

She pulled his head down to hers, her fingers threading through dark, silky hair. She lifted her face to his and angled it to try and kiss him. She felt so awkward. She aimed for his mouth, but ended up bumping his nose, his chin. She pulled back, letting him go. This was ridiculous. No doubt he'd expected her to sashay up to him, throw him down on the sofa and seduce him into mindless ecstasy. Well, he'd be waiting.

Her voice was stiff with humiliation. This was exactly what she'd feared. 'I'm sorry. I haven't…done this in a while. I think you expect me to be something…more than I am.'

She turned to go but he caught her wrist and pulled her back. She fell against him, caught off-balance. With the practised ease which she lacked and so envied, he immediately cradled the back of her head with a big hand, the other holding her close against him.

'Not at all. I just wanted to be sure you were ready for this.'

'Maybe I'm not, after all,' she breathed up, mesmerised by his eyes.

'I think you are.' And then he bent his head and kissed her, exactly how she'd been aching to be kissed since the last time. Both hands now threaded through her hair, messing it up, cradling her head. Her hands rested on his chest and wound higher until they were tight around his neck. They barely paused for breath; there was no awkwardness now. First their kiss was slow, sensual, a tentative touching of tongues, tasting. Then it developed into full-on passion, igniting an inferno between them.

Somehow, Alana didn't know how, Pascal had manoeuvered them and now her back was against a wall. He lifted his head. One hand was high on the wall behind her, the other resting on her hip. She felt as boneless as a rag doll. She looked up, her eyes glazed, her lips plump and tingling.

His index-finger traced around her jaw and down to the top button of her shirt. Her heart stopped and kick-started again. Faster.

'Do you have any idea what this outfit has been doing to me since I saw you arrive in it?'

She shook her head. All she knew was that she wanted to be out of it. As soon as possible.

He started to undo her tie. 'As much as this turns me on,' he said gruffly, 'I think I'm going to have to burn it.'

'I have ten more at home,' Alana said matter of factly, distractedly.

He threw it aside and it landed in a sliver of dark colour on the wooden floor. 'Then it'll be a bonfire.'

His fingers were at her buttons now. She tipped her head back to give him access, and she felt him drop his head and press a kiss to the exposed, delicate skin of her throat. Alana moaned softly. She was in a sensual land that she'd never thought she'd experience. She'd heard other women talk of lust and chemical attraction, and had always secretly disbelieved them or thought it was overrated. Now…she *knew*.

She could sense Pascal's growing impatience when he

couldn't undo any more buttons as the dress got in the way. He growled, 'How do you get this thing off?'

Alana stood and turned around to face the wall. 'The zip. At the back.'

She could feel it whisper down, and then he turned her round again. Bending to take her mouth with his, she could feel his hands go to the shoulders of her dress and push it down; it snagged on her hips, and then his hands were there and pushing it off completely until it fell at her feet, a pool of pleated black.

She brought her hands to the bottom of his sweater to pull it up. He lifted his arms and pulled it off the whole way, and then he stood in front of her, bare chested. She could feel her eyes widening as she took in the bronzed magnificence. Whorls of dark hair dusted his pectorals and then met in a silky line that descended down and into the waist of his low-slung jeans which barely clung to lean hips.

Heat. All Alana could think of was *heat*.

He pulled her into him and she gloried in the sensation of his bare chest, running her hands round his back, feeling the satin-smooth olive skin, warm beneath her fingers. He gathered her close and his mouth closed over the beating, throbbing pulse at her neck; his hands travelled down to her bottom and caressed it before searching further and finding the bare skin at the top of her thighs over her stockings. He jerked back and looked down, eyes glittering, breath coming harshly.

*'Mon Dieu.'*

'What?' she asked uncertainly, feeling exposed.

He just shook his head and a huge grin split his face. 'Stockings. Proper stockings. And suspenders.' What was turning him on even more was the suspicion that she dressed like this all the time, that it hadn't been just for him.

He looked at her then. 'I knew that underneath all that starch was someone earthy, sensual…'

He kissed her, and she felt his hands undoing the rest of the buttons on her shirt, the slightly cooler air hitting her torso as he pulled it apart. He looked at her for a long moment before pushing it off, down her arms, until it too joined her dress on the floor.

The carnal appreciation in his gaze made her throb in response. She was glad now that bizarrely she'd always had an instinctive desire for nice underwear, although she hadn't indulged it while married, as Ryan had mocked her for trying to be sexy whenever she did. Her breasts were straining against the satin cups of her bra, peaks tingling painfully. Pascal pushed one strap down over her shoulder and dragged down the cup, baring one pale breast to his gaze...and mouth.

He whispered in her ear, 'Remember what I said before?'

She nodded jerkily, anticipation lasering through her veins.

Then he bent his head and blew softly and enticed, before flicking out his tongue to taste and then drawing that tight, extended peak into his mouth. Alana's head fell back. She couldn't stop the moan, and wondered at this woman she didn't recognise.

As Pascal suckled, a tight spiral of intense sensation connected directly with Alana's groin. She found herself pressing closer, seeking, wanting more, arching her back. He had taken down the other cup, so now both her breasts were bared, upthrust and framed by the satin black material.

He was torturing her with his mouth. She couldn't breathe. He reached down, lifted one leg and hooked it around his thigh. His other hand was on the leg that was barely able to keep her standing. His fingers danced over the suspenders; she felt him snap open the ties, then smooth around to cup the cheek of her bottom before slipping his hand between her legs.

She stopped breathing entirely for a long moment as he pushed her panties aside and slid his finger into her, into a caress so intimate that she would have closed her legs if she'd been able to. He was relentless, his mouth on her breasts, his finger sliding in and out, until finally, as if he'd been teasing her, he found the centre of where she throbbed unmercifully and, with one flick of his thumb, she came violently. She could only cling to him as the sensation ripped through her body in case she'd be swept away too.

Her leg that was lifted fell. She couldn't quite believe what had just happened. A bit like chemical attraction; she'd read about it, heard about it. But amazingly…

'Alana, was that your first orgasm?' He sounded slightly stunned, and Alana cringed inwardly at how gauche she must seem.

He stood upright and let her settle against him, cradling her with a disconcerting level of tenderness. As if he could sense her turmoil, he tipped her head back. 'No, don't do that. You're amazingly responsive, but it's nothing to be embarrassed about. It's a compliment.'

She looked at him shyly, mortified. 'I'm—'

'Don't say it.' He shook his head. His expression was enigmatic. 'You were married; did you never…?'

She shook her head quickly, her body still pulsing in the aftermath, making her feel a little out of this world. Spaced out. 'My husband never…made me feel like that. We didn't sleep together for the last three years of our marriage.'

'And you were married for…'

'Five years.' Unwelcome reality was trickling back in. Alana resented the questions now; she didn't want to think of Ryan. This was her new start for herself. Ryan was in the past.

'Alana—'

She pressed a finger to Pascal's mouth and could feel his breath feather there, could feel a delicious tightening in her belly. 'Please. I don't want to talk about it, OK?' He didn't say anything for a long moment, and then finally he nodded.

Alana gave a huge sigh of relief, and then yelped as Pascal lifted her into his arms against his chest.

'Time to go somewhere more comfortable, I think. Much as I could take you standing against that wall right now, I'll resist the temptation.'

She buried her head in his shoulder as he climbed the stairs and shouldered his way into his room.

A part of her wanted nothing more than that carnality, but another part of her was grateful that he was being so considerate.

He looked down at her briefly, his face tight with need. 'Is this OK?'

She nodded. She knew one thing for sure for the first time in ages. 'Yes.'

Alana woke to a delicious sensation of someone running a finger up and down her bare spine in a tingling caress. Pascal. Warmth flooded her even as she registered aches and pleasurable pains all over her body. She opened one eye to see him smiling at her, looking clean, vital and very awake. He smelt fresh, delicious. And sexy. Heat flooded her belly.

The previous night came back in Technicolor: the pathetic fight she'd put up before giving in, the amount of times they'd made love, the amount of times she'd reached ecstasy because of him.

He bent his head and his mouth hovered near her ear. 'No regrets and no recriminations. We agreed, remember?'

Alana turned her face into the pillow so he wouldn't see her blushing. She just nodded into the pillow. She heard a soft, sexy chuckle and then felt a playful swat on her bottom. The bed dipped and she could feel him standing up.

'Come on; my car will be here for you in half an hour, and if you're anything like the rest of your species, you'll be struggling to get ready in time.'

Alana lifted her head with a squeak. 'Half an hour?' She cursed under her breath and went to get up, and realised that she had no cover, as her clothes had practically melted off her last night in the heat of passion that had consumed them. She was stuck. Pascal stood between her and the door from where she could get to her own bedroom. She was not ready to parade around naked in broad daylight.

He watched, amused, as she pulled the sheet from the bed and wrapped it around her before getting up and trailing it after her.

Before she was clear of him, he caught her and pulled her against him. He pressed a hot kiss to her mouth. 'Take the sheet for now, but I'll have you walking around naked in no time.'

'Never…'

He kissed her again, and suddenly the vortex was opening up around them, and in a shamingly small amount of time Alana knew she would be saying yes to anything, even going to work naked. But then he drew back, showing her that ultimately he was in control, whereas she was not. He pushed her gently towards her room.

Under the powerful spray of her shower, Alana hugged her arms around herself and gave into the stream of images. She groaned out loud as she remembered one moment, half in mortification, half in a state of arousal, even now. Pascal had been poised above her, skin gleaming, slick with sweat, his erection nudging her moist entrance. As if he'd been testing her again, he'd waited until her nerves had been screaming for release. She'd arched up to him, willing him to impale her, but he'd waited until she'd brokenly begged him. And then he'd slid into her slowly, deeply.

With a curt flick of her wrist Alana turned the shower to cold and endured it for a minute. Anything to dampen her flaming hormones.

\* \* \*

At the match later Pascal came and found her at half time, and took her by the hand. She was distracted; she'd been trying to set up an interview for after the match with the England manager.

'Pascal, I'm working, you can't just walk up and drag me away,' she said with a mixture of reproach and breathless anticipation.

He ignored her and took her down into long corridors before ducking into a room full of equipment. He closed the door behind them.

Still holding her hand, he pulled her to him. She was helpless not to respond, her body welcoming his heady proximity. How quickly she'd become consumed by him. Alarm bells weren't just ringing, they were now joined by sirens and flashing lights.

With quick hands, he undid her ponytail and pocketed the band.

'Hey!'

Then he put two hands in her hair and mussed it up. He looked at her critically. 'Much better. And now…'

'Now what?'

'Now this.' He hauled her into him and kissed her deeply, with barely checked passion. She wound her arms around his waist and found her hands lifting his shirt from his trousers, searching for and finding that smooth, taut flesh where the small of his back curved out to firm buttocks. Warmth flooded her. He was opening the buttons of her shirt; she'd tried to put on her tie that morning but he'd kept taking it off her. She could feel the air on her heated skin as he opened her shirt and palmed her breast, her nipple aching against the confines of her bra. She pressed a feverish mouth against his throat.

And then suddenly the spell was broken as someone tried to come in the door behind them. Pascal said something quickly in Italian and started to do up her buttons again. Alana didn't know how she was going to be able to go back out there and string two words together.

Her brain was mush for the rest of the match and the ensuing interviews, but somehow she managed to keep it together. Pascal was waiting for her, exactly like he'd been waiting and watching that first day in Dublin. Only now... A wave of heat engulfed her...only now it was totally different. She was different.

Her crew feigned extreme lack of interest in the fact that Pascal Lévêque was hovering like a bodyguard. But once the last interview was done, and she'd been given the all clear from the Dublin studio, effectively the rest of the weekend was hers.

In the back of Pascal's car a short time later, he pulled her over so she was practically on his lap. She'd given up trying to pull away and retain a more dignified position for the sake of the driver. He pressed a kiss to the underside of her wrist and looked up at her.

'Are you glad to be here now?'

Alana looked down at him and felt the earth move bizarrely beneath her feet even though they were in a moving vehicle. Something very suspicious tightened her chest. She nodded, because she had to admit it. 'Yes. I am glad.' She bent her head and pressed a kiss to his mouth, revelling in the freedom she had to do this. They'd achieved an immediate level of intimacy that would be frightening if she thought about it too closely.

She was embarking on an affair with a world-renowned playboy and that was going to be her protection: at no point would she be deluded. At no point would there be talk of love, marriage. It would end when it would end. And she'd take the gift of herself that he'd given back to her, like a guilty, delicious secret. That was all she wanted. This was all she wanted.

Later that evening Alana took one last look at her reflection and turned to leave the room, but just then her door opened. Pascal stopped dead for a moment, his gaze raking her up and down, and then he clapped his hand over his eyes. 'I can't believe it.'

Alana felt like a fool. She knew she shouldn't have worn the dress—it was ridiculous, too tight, too revealing. 'Look, I can change, I'm not even that comfortable.'

Pascal wasn't moving.

She took a hesitant step forward. 'What, what is it? Is it really that bad?'

Alana tried to look back at the mirror self-consciously when she heard something suspiciously like a grunt coming from Pascal.

He'd taken his hand down and was laughing. Then he stopped and walked towards her. 'I'm sorry. I couldn't help it. It was the shock of seeing so much exposed flesh at once.'

Alana all at once felt like laughing and angry. She picked up a small cushion from the chair beside her and threw it at him, but he caught it deftly and kept coming. Dressed in a tuxedo, with his hair still damp from the shower, he was magnificent.

She had to speak to try and negate the effect he had on her, the way his teasing wound through her and impacted a place that was so deep, so vulnerable.

'I'm going to change right now; I knew this dress was a mistake.'

She went to undo the zip that was under her arm, and Pascal reached her and captured her hand. 'Don't you dare. That dress is beautiful.'

Alana's face flamed. 'It's not. It's too—'

'So why did you bring it, then?'

She couldn't answer. He walked her over to the full-length mirror and stood her in front of him. His hands rested on her hips. She could feel him, tall and hard and lean behind her, and it was so seductive.

'Look at yourself.'

Alana closed her eyes, her cheeks still scarlet. She shook her head. 'I hate looking at myself.'

'Alana, *look* at yourself.'

Something in his voice made her open her eyes, and she immediately looked at him through the mirror. She could feel him sigh behind her.

'Not at me, at yourself.'

With extreme reluctance, she did. She saw the black silk dress that was cut on the bias and fell to just below her knees in an asymmetric line. She saw one shoulder, pale and bared, and just a hint of a curve of her breast. She saw the strap that held the dress up over her other shoulder with its flamboyant red-silk flower, a splash of vibrant colour.

'Now, what's wrong with this picture?'

Alana groaned inwardly. This was so embarrassing. She would bet a million dollars that not one of his previous lovers had had to be reassured about a dress before.

She tried to turn. 'Look, it's nothing, I'm sorry. Let's just go, shall we?'

He wouldn't let her. He held her fast, and something in the air changed. It became electric.

'You're beautiful, Alana. This dress is beautiful on you. It's not too revealing. In fact,' he growled with mock lasciviousness, 'it's not revealing enough.'

He turned her then to face him, his hands warm on her shoulders. She could feel her breasts peak against the silk of the dress.

He tipped up her chin so she couldn't avoid his eyes. 'What did he do to you, Alana? I bet you weren't always like this.'

Alana struggled not to let the tears brighten her eyes, but there was a lump in her throat. She shook her head. 'No, I wasn't. He just…he just made me feel cheap. That's all.'

She pulled free of his arms and looked at her watch. 'We should really go.'

He heard the emotion in her voice and watched her precede him out of the room, the dress emphasising her gently curved shape, the jut of her rounded bottom. He could recall only too clearly the thrust of her breasts against his chest.

He stalled a moment before following her out. She was so totally different from any woman he'd known before that he couldn't quite begin to rationalise how she made him feel. Physically, he burned for her. Earlier at the match he'd quite literally *had* to see her, touch her at half time or he'd felt he would have gone insane. She'd been preoccupied. First of all, he wasn't used to any woman being preoccupied around him, and secondly, he wasn't used not to being in complete control with his lovers. They turned him on, yes, that was what he chose them for, but never to the extent that he felt with this woman. This was something different.

He straightened his cuffs before walking out, uncomfortably aware of his near-constant state of arousal. She was just different because she wasn't one of the polished socialites that littered his social scene, who threw themselves at him, that was all. It was still just an affair, and he'd no doubt that he'd soon look at her and wonder what he'd been hot and bothered about.

A little later, in the exclusive hotel which was hosting his bank's lavish charity-ball, Pascal felt extremely hot and bothered. Alana was generating a veritable tsunami of attention in her sexy dress. After having spent the last two weeks trying to get her out of her buttoned-up uniform, now he wanted to march her right out of there and make her change back into it.

Clamping her to his side was a need born out of a violent emotion that he'd never felt before as acquaintance after acquaintance came up under the pretext of talking business, whereupon they did nothing but stare at Alana. She seemed oblivious, but Pascal was too inured to women and their wily ways. And he was all too aware of how beguiling her natural beauty was to these men, who were jaded and cynical. As jaded and cynical as he was. Was he no better than these men? He'd just seen her first. All sorts of conflicting, unsavoury thoughts were being unleashed within him. Not least of which was the sensation that perhaps he'd been fooled, fooled by her act, her apparent vulnerability. *How* could she really be so different?

He dragged her attention back from where she was looking in awe at the room around them, and muttered something about getting drinks. He saw a flash of uncertainty in her eyes and ignored it, and the feeling it generated through him. He needed space.

Alana looked to where Pascal was cutting a swathe through the glittering crowd. She couldn't help but notice the intense interest he generated among every cluster of women in the room, who also followed his progress with avid attention. Some of them turned then to look at her, and she felt extremely self-conscious. Trying to shrug off the immediate insecurity that their looks generated, she walked to where ornate doors led out to a small, idyllic garden. Even though it was cool, one or two people mingled outside. The hotel was pure opulence, one of the oldest and grandest in Rome, situated with a view of the Spanish Steps.

She couldn't help but think of similar situations with Ryan. He'd always dumped her as soon as they got in the door and made straight for the bar. Invariably she'd be left on her own all evening and would return home alone, only to wake up in the morning and find that he hadn't even returned. She'd stopped worrying about his whereabouts soon into the marriage when it had become clear he'd never seemed to miss her.

She rubbed her arms distractedly, as she had that sensation of someone walking over her grave.

'*Bella.*'

Alana jumped and turned to see a tall man standing beside her, looking her up and down. She looked nervously over his shoulder back into the room, but couldn't see Pascal. She smiled tightly. 'I'm sorry, I don't speak Italian; I'm just waiting for someone, actually.'

'Then it's lucky that I speak English. You are a very beautiful woman.'

Alana blushed. 'That's very…nice of you to say.' The man was attractive in a heavy-set kind of way, but there was something faintly menacing about him. He'd moved subtly and now he effectively blocked her from the room. In order to move, Alana would have to push past him or go into the garden. She didn't want to retreat to a dark area where he might follow her.

'Please.' He held out a hand. 'Can I know your name?'

Alana sent up a silent prayer for Pascal to find her. Where *was* he? She couldn't ignore the man, as that would be unaccountably rude. So she shook his hand very perfunctorily and whipped hers back before he could clasp it. 'Alana Cusack; I'm very pleased to meet you. Now, please, my friend will be looking for me.' *Except patently he wasn't.* A very familiar feeling of pain clutched her deep down inside.

She went to move past the man, but he stopped her with an arm. Alana flinched back from the contact.

His voice now held a distinctly threatening tone. 'But I haven't told you my name yet, and your accent—where are you from? It is so pretty.'

Alana was beginning to feel desperate. Even though Ryan had never physically harmed her, the latent threat had always been there, and now the memory was making her feel panicky. 'Look, I don't mean to be rude, but I don't really want to know your name, OK? Now, I'm sorry, but would you *please* get out of my way?'

After a long, tense moment, he stepped back with hands held high and spread. 'Go then, if you want, it's your loss.'

Alana seized the opportunity and fled. Her heart was hammering, and she had an awful, sick feeling in her chest, an overwhelming sensation of foreboding. She pushed through the crowd and then she saw Pascal, and the whole room tilted crazily, the chatter dulling to a faint roaring in her ears.

He was at the bar, talking to a woman. He didn't look as if he was in a hurry to go anywhere, much less to look for Alana. The woman was stunningly beautiful—blonde, tall, slim, in a sparkling gown with a thigh-high slit that was being provocatively displayed. She had a hand on Pascal's waist and was leaning in, her whole body arching seductively into his. His head was bent towards hers as if she were telling him something intimate.

It all hit Alana at once, and again she felt acutely self-conscious in her revealing dress. She hated the compulsion that had led her to wear it now. But, worse than that, she'd let herself be taken in *again* by a man who lived his life searching for the next thrill, the next pleasure-point. The next adoring female. She could see all too well, in a room like this, how she must have been such a novelty. The innocent Irish cailín. And then, like watching a car crash in slow motion, she saw Pascal's hand go to where the woman's rested on his waist. He was about to thread his fingers through hers, lift her hand to his mouth. Alana knew it. But just before she could turn away her humiliation became complete. They both turned, as if they could sense her watching them.

The glittering, too-bright icy-blue gaze of the woman was mocking, triumphant. Pascal's was… She didn't wait to find out. Turning, Alana stumbled and pushed through the crowd until she was finally free of the room and burst out into the spacious and hushed lobby. She walked quickly to the door on jelly legs, where a doorman rushed to open it for her.

# CHAPTER FIVE

ALANA stood on the steps, shivering.

'You would like me to get you a taxi, madam?'

'Yes, please,' Alana said gratefully to the nice doorman. She had no idea where she would go—all her stuff was at Pascal's—but she just wanted away from here.

'She doesn't need a taxi, she's with me. Can you send for my driver, please?' a familiar deep voice, throbbing with anger, came from behind her and she stiffened in rejection.

A harsh hand on her arm pulled her round. She met furious dark eyes, and everything in her rebelled against *his* anger. The fact that the doorman had already scurried off to do his bidding made things even worse.

'I believe that I just ordered a taxi; thanks all the same for the offer of the lift.'

'What the hell just happened back there?'

'Why, I believe what just happened is that you saw a better option and decided to pursue it, leaving me at the mercy of a...a creepy, slimy lounge-lizard.'

His hand tightened on her arm. 'What are you talking about? Did someone come on to you? Did someone do something to you?'

'No,' she dismissed him furiously, while trying to shake him off unsuccessfully. 'Not that you would have noticed anyway. But, thanks, you've saved me going back in to look for you. If you could give me the keys to your apartment, I'd appreciate it; I'll get my things and be gone by the time you get back. No doubt you'll be wanting the place to yourself tonight?'

'And why would that be?' His voice was arctic, but Alana was on fire.

'Do you really need me to spell it out, Pascal? I thought you were more sophisticated than that.' She berated herself bitterly now for having allowed herself to be seduced by him.

'Apparently not so sophisticated that I can go to the bar to get a drink for my date and turn around to find she has disappeared, only to find her again and have her run from the room as if I'd chased her out myself.'

He'd been looking for her? A reflex to stop, to apologise, was quashed as she remembered the woman. They'd looked far too cosy. She'd only known Pascal two weeks. Did she really think she could trust him? Her astounding naïvety mocked her mercilessly.

'Your companion might have another impression. She seemed to think that you were quite interested in what she had to offer.'

Pascal could recall only too noxiously what the British model Cecilia Hampton had been offering. She'd all but wrapped herself around him like a clinging vine, and had spoken in an absurdly quiet, jarring little-girl voice—a well-worn ploy to get a man to come closer, whereupon she'd all but thrust her enormous fake bosom in his face. He'd been feeling foolish ever since he'd stalked away from Alana to get drinks, and had turned back to get her, imagining all the predatory males in the room moving in on her, but she'd disappeared.

His car drew up at that moment and, heaving a sigh of relief, he hurried Alana down the steps and into the back, making her slide along the seat and getting in beside her, not giving her a chance to get out. Or say a thing.

In the back of the car Alana ripped her arm from Pascal's grasp, her skin hot and tingling. 'How dare you? I want you to let me out this minute. I'll get a cab.'

She sat forward and opened her mouth to speak to the driver, but Pascal hauled her over and she lay sprawled inelegantly against him. With his other hand he flicked a switch and the privacy window slid up with a hiss.

The air was electric around them. Alana was very aware of how she lay practically across his lap, in a pose of supplication that galled her. His body was tense and taut, and unmistakably hard. It made her feel sick, that he could so easily transfer his desire from one to another.

'Isn't there something wrong with this picture?' she gritted out, holding herself as tense and as far away as possible.

'Yes,' Pascal ground out. 'You're wearing far too many clothes for my liking and I want you *now*.'

Alana tried to pull free, but he was remorseless and held her still. 'You don't want me, you want *her*.'

In an instant Pascal had shifted and lifted Alana with an ease that shocked her. She found herself straddling his lap, knees pressed either side of his powerful thighs. His hands were on her waist, holding her captive. A wave of anger and humiliation at her own helpless response, her lack of strength, drove her to try and move but she couldn't.

Her arms were rigid, either side of Pascal's shoulders on the seat behind them. With his hands firmly on her waist he shifted her slightly so that she could feel where his erection strained between them against the confines of his trousers. A rush of desire made her suck in a betraying breath. And then his hands came up to her dress, to undo the clasp hidden underneath the flower. If he undid that, her dress would fall to her waist.

'Don't you dare.' She caught his hands, but he swatted hers away with ease. He undid her dress and it fell. Alana caught it. The motion of the car made her fall against him, and made the apex between her legs grind into Pascal's hardness. She could hear his breath coming harshly, see the colour slash across his cheekbones. She felt sick inside, knowing that he could just as easily be doing this with any other woman.

She heard him sigh, and he looked up at her with a curiously unguarded expression. She was caught by it.

'Alana, please believe me: if I were in the unfortunate position of having Cecilia Hampton straddle my lap right now, I can assure you that she would not be feeling what you're feeling.'

He snaked a hand around the back of her neck. Alana tried to hold herself stiff, but it was too difficult. His voice was low, reasonable, and oh, so sexy. 'You'd disappeared when I went looking for you, so I went back to wait at the bar, thinking you'd come find me there. Cecilia approached me. If you'd watched for another few seconds before running out, you would have seen me extricate myself from her extremely unwelcome embrace.'

Alana looked down at him. He looked sincere. Had she read it wrong? She found herself wanting to believe him so much. And that was beyond scary in its implications. But right now she could avoid thinking about it without a huge amount of effort. The need consuming her, consuming the air around them, was too great. Desire flowed, hot and urgent, between them. This was all-encompassing, and she had to give into it and deal with the fallout later.

Pascal slowly moved his hand from the back of her neck, over her shoulder and down to her hands. He exerted a little bit of pressure and Alana let him pull her hands away, giving in to a need too great. Her dress fell to her waist, baring her breasts. She put her hands back onto the seat behind Pascal. He took her face in his hands and kissed her softly, reverently. It made something hard melt inside her. She sank into him, found her hips moving sinuously against his. Urgency rose. His kiss became more forceful. He dragged his mouth away and held the weight of one breast in his hand before flicking out a tongue and laving the distended peak. Alana's back arched.

She pressed kisses feverishly to his face, mouth, neck, her hands seeking to rip open his shirt. Buttons popped and his bow tie disappeared down into the cracks between the seats. She blindly sought his belt buckle and opened it impatiently.

'You're like a fever in my blood, Alana. There's no one else I want.'

His words set her aflame even more, and she bent to kiss him again. He lifted her slightly and she braced her hands against his shoulders. She bit her lip as she heard his zip come down, and as he pulled his trousers down with a rough urgency. Then he settled her back and she almost cried out at the sensation of his hard, virile, unsheathed heat, *right there*.

He lifted her dress at her waist, and she heard fabric rip as he brought two hands to the side of her knickers and pulled. He pressed a kiss to her throat as she felt the material being pulled away. 'I'm not sorry and I'll buy you new ones.'

She didn't care. She wanted him inside her, right now. The ache was killing her.

As if he heard her silent plea, he lifted her again, and she could feel his hand on himself as he guided his rigid length to the apex of her thighs. He slid in easily, and as Alana sank down onto him, he surged upwards. She was so turned on, and the sensation was so shockingly thrilling, that she came right there and then, her inner muscles clamping around him in a series of minor convulsions.

She dropped her head into his shoulder. He was still rigid within her, filling her. 'Oh God, I'm sorry…' She was breathing heavily.

He pulled her back, tipped her head up, pressed a kiss to her mouth, slid his tongue between her soft lips. She could feel him stir within her, and inexplicably she could feel herself start to respond again, not being allowed to fall back to earth; she was kept on a high plateau of sensation that threatened to go even higher.

'We've only just started.'

With a slow, burning intensity, Pascal moved within her like a devil magician. He brought her to the edge only to stop, then start again. In a fever of prolonged ecstasy, skin slick with sweat, it was only when he knew he couldn't hold back that he allowed free rein to his movements, which became urgent. His big hands moulded her back, held her hips steady. Alana was beyond words. Everything in her was reverent, the orgasm that broke through her just before his was so powerful that she had to keep her eyes locked on Pascal's or she would have disintegrated into pieces.

Pascal had never felt anything like it. He'd almost have believed that she hadn't climaxed, if he hadn't felt her body contracting powerfully around his. But she'd done it with such quiet intensity that it had made his own completion burst up in a never-ending stream of exquisite pleasure. Only her biting her lip at the zenith of sensation had shown any of her internal experience.

Alana shook all over. Pascal pulled her into his chest and cradled her against him. They were still joined intimately, and at that moment she couldn't ever imagine being separated from this man. She'd never felt like this with her husband, not even in the early days of their marriage when she'd had so many hopes and dreams of a happy future.

Something extraordinary had just happened, and she hated to admit it.

\* \* \*

When they reached his apartment, Pascal carried her straight up to his bathroom and ran them a bath. Then they made love. Again. And now she lay here, blissed out. Replete. Complete.

She heard a movement and looked up. Pascal was holding out a big robe.

'Come on, or you'll turn into a prune.'

Something in his eyes made her hold back a quick, joky comment. She stood up and reached for the robe, only to have him pull it back from her reach.

'Pascal, come on.' She groaned and immediately went to cover her breasts. She was totally exposed in the low lighting of the intimate bathroom. And it was silly to feel this way when they'd just made love, first in the back of his car and then in the bath. She flushed.

'Let your hands down. Please.' His voice sounded rough. 'I want to look at you, Alana—will you let me look at you? As you are?'

Fear and embarrassment gave way to something else. The desire in his eyes emboldened her. She carefully and slowly climbed out of the bath and stood beside it. She dropped her arms and watched as his eyes travelled down, resting and dwelling on parts of her body that she'd certainly never inspected so intensely herself.

After a long, long minute his eyes met hers again. They were dark. He stepped forward and put the robe around her, drying her, before slipping her arms into the sleeves and tying it securely around her waist. He smoothed back her damp hair and ran a finger down her cheek.

'I could quite easily have you again right now, on the floor... And all sorts of other images came into my mind as I looked at you.' Pascal wrestled for a moment inwardly with the very real and disturbing reality that he could take her again right now. The knowledge made him cautious. 'But there's time...'

'Time,' Alana said stupidly, suddenly wanting very much

instead that they could make love on the floor right now. She had an erotic flash of an image: kneeling at his feet and taking him into her mouth. The shocking heat that inflamed her made her feel weak. Where had that desire come from? She'd never even done that with Ryan. She'd never even thought that she found it sexy. But the thought of driving Pascal to the edge of all endurance was intoxicating in the extreme.

'Yes, time. Let's eat and have some wine.' He cut through the fevered images in her wanton imagination and pushed her towards the bathroom door, and then out and down the stairs to the sitting room. A bottle of wine sat open with two glasses. Alana felt stone-cold sober all of a sudden, which wasn't surprising as she hadn't drunk all evening, but bizarrely she also felt drunk, heady…something very nebulous and disturbing.

He poured wine into their glasses and busied himself with something at the oven. Although Alana was in a robe, Pascal wore faded jeans and a plain shirt that was haphazardly buttoned, showing the light smattering of hair on his chest and a sliver of hard-muscled, olive-skinned belly. Alana took a quick sip of wine. He really did have the honed body of an athlete—again something niggled at her about that, but it was wispy and eluded her.

'Look,' she started nervously. 'I'm sorry about…running out like that. I'm not normally so dramatic.'

Pascal closed the oven door and slanted her a look before taking a sip of wine from his own glass.

Alana flushed. 'We should still be there. Didn't you have to make some kind of speech?'

Pascal shrugged noncommittally. 'My assistant did it. It's no big deal, really; I wouldn't have even been here necessarily if it hadn't been for the match happening on the same day. It was an opportunity to drum up publicity and kill two birds with one stone. But, no.' He smiled disarmingly. 'I would much prefer to be here with you.'

She flushed again, unused to being flattered. 'Well. Thank you. Next time—'

She stopped abruptly, her eyes flying to his with a sickening feeling as she realised what she'd been about to say—she'd been about to imply that there would *be* a next time.

'That is, I don't mean—'

Pascal hushed her and came round the counter, pulling her into him. 'Next time I'm not going to let you out of my sight, so there will be no room for any confusion or misinterpretation, OK?'

Her mouth was dry and she just nodded.

He let her go and moved back, smiling easily, charmingly, and her world tilted all over again. 'Now, how about you tell me about this lounge-lizard of yours?'

Alana shuddered delicately at the memory, realising that it had shaken her more than she cared to admit, but talking about it would lessen it. She told Pascal and acted out his slimy manoeuvres, and by the time she'd finished they were both laughing, and Pascal admitted that he knew exactly who she was talking about. Apparently the man was famous for pouncing on vulnerable-looking women. Their easy intimacy and Pascal's ability to make her feel protected, to make her feel like she could *trust* him, was sucking Alana into a veritable whirlpool that she feared it would be nigh impossible to climb back out of.

The following evening, as Alana looked at the Italian capital grow smaller and smaller beneath her, she got hot in the face again thinking of the previous night. The erotic fantasy she'd had in the bathroom had become a reality. Pascal had let her push him to the edge of his endurance. She groaned inwardly; she seemed to be in a permanent state of heat since she met him.

She was alone on his private jet on her way back to Dublin. He was taking a commercial flight back to Paris, and he hadn't taken no for an answer when she'd objected. He'd flown her to him, and now he was flying her home. Just like that. As if flying someone on a private jet was banal, ordinary. Easy. And she had to concede, for someone like him who strode through life and got what they wanted with a click of their fingers, of course it was easy. Accolades, money, women, beautiful houses—easy come, easy go. And she'd put herself firmly in that category, made no bones about the fact that she was fine with that.

She finally turned away from the view and recalled the stern set of his features as he'd sent her off, having insisted on accompanying her to the airport. They'd had their first row, of sorts. Except it had been more like a non-row. Alana still couldn't quite figure what had happened but all she knew was that he hadn't been happy.

They'd woken late, well into the early afternoon. Pascal had insisted that she see something of Rome, and had taken her to the nearby Trevi Fountain and then to a tiny restaurant tucked away from the hordes of tourists. The food had been sublime, authentic Italian cuisine at its best. The experience had been intimate, the table so small that their legs had been all but entwined underneath, and it had been easier for their hands to stay linked, too, separating only when the food arrived.

It was when they'd got back to his apartment so that Alana could pack; they'd been standing in the kitchen and she'd been watching Pascal percolate some coffee. He'd turned round and said easily, 'There's so much more you should see. But we can do it again.'

Alana had immediately reacted to his words at a very deep, visceral level, an instant negation of something very fleeting and wishful rising up inside her. 'Oh, well, yes. I'm sure I'll be back at some stage.'

It was the way she'd said *'I'* that got his attention, and she knew it. Even though he said nothing—at first. And then he did say, 'I meant when you come back here with me.'

Alana took the coffee he handed her and walked away into the living room, holding the cup between suddenly chilled hands. She schooled her features and turned back round to face him, forcing her voice to sound as casual as she could. 'You really don't have to say that, you know.'

He took a sip of coffee, his eyes narrowed disconcertingly on her face. She was glad that he was still behind the island in the kitchen.

'And what's that supposed to mean?'

Alana gave a little laugh, which sounded fake to her ears. 'I mean, you don't have to do this...reassurance thing. I really don't expect you to make me feel like you want me to come back...' Her words trailed off, diminishing some of the vehemence with which she'd started the statement.

He walked round the island, ridiculously small coffee cup in one hand, his other in the pocket of his jeans. He looked astoundingly gorgeous in a dark sweater. Unconsciously, Alana backed away.

'Believe me,' he said throatily, 'the only thing I want to make you feel right now involves a soft surface and no clothing in our way.'

Alana gulped and took a quick swig of coffee.

'Look,' she said weakly, 'all I'm saying is that I know what this is and I'm fine with that. Really.'

'And what would *that* be?'

She shrugged one shoulder; they were still doing a bit of a backward dance around the room, she backing, and he advancing.

'It's an affair. A fling.'

His eyebrows raised high. 'Oh, so that's what this is?'

Alana winced. No doubt his other lovers were far too experienced and suave to put a name on their experience with him. Suddenly she felt anger rise up. Why was he being so obtuse? Surely she was doing him a favour? She stopped backing away and put her coffee cup down carefully on the low table by the sofa.

She straightened and folded her arms. 'Look, that's exactly what it is. We both know that. I'd prefer if we could just be honest about it. What I'm saying to you is that I don't need to be given any kind of platitudes. I'm not going to be clingy or want anything more. If you said to me right now that this is over, and thanks but goodbye, I'd have no problem walking out of here.'

Pascal had gone very still, his eyes very black. No doubt he wasn't used to lovers calling the shots, Alana thought cynically. And why did her flip words cause an ache somewhere in the region of her chest? She pushed it aside. The truth was this: Pascal was not a man she could trust in a million years. And she'd vowed to herself never to trust again. Never to be so silly, naïve.

Pascal put down his coffee cup, too, and walked towards her slowly. Alana stood her ground, but had the impression that she'd woken a sleeping dragon.

'I'll admit that your honesty is both tantalising and refreshing.'

'It is?' she asked.

Pascal nodded. He was close enough to touch now.

'Yes. We both know that when the time comes, we'll walk away without a backward glance, happy with what we've had.'

'Exactly.' Alana nodded vehemently. 'I don't mean to sound...crass, it's just that I've been married. I've had that experience and I never, ever want to go near it again. Not even in the form of a tenuous commitment—and I know you're not even offering that.' She stopped and cursed herself; she sounded like a bumbling idiot. 'What I'm trying to say is that I'm not looking for anything. I know you're a playboy.'

His eyes flashed, and Alana's insides clenched painfully

but she ploughed on. 'I'm not expecting anything more. I can't begin to tell you how comfortable I am with that.'

'A no-strings, no-consequences affair—we both walk away when we get bored.'

She nodded. She knew that time wouldn't be far off. A man of Pascal's voracious tastes wouldn't be content with someone like her for long. Not when there were other, more beautiful women waiting in the wings.

He came very close and snaked a hand round the back of her head. His eyes were still dark, unreadable, and his jaw had a rigidity to it that made Alana instinctively want to smooth it, relax it.

'Well, then, seeing as how it's doubtful you will ever be back here with me, now that the sands of time are slipping away from us, we should make the most of here and now, *n'est-ce pas?*'

'What do you mean?'

'What I mean, Alana—' his voice had a hard edge '—is that we're wasting too much time talking when we could be saying goodbye to Rome and this weekend in a very satisfactory way.'

He kissed her for a long, drugging moment, hauling her whole body against his. When he pulled back, and Alana fought to regain her breath, she said, 'But your plane...we have to leave.'

He shook his head, eyes flashing dangerously. 'That's the beauty of being a playboy—my crew are very used to last-minute changes.'

Alana felt a knife skewer her inside, so hurt for a moment that she felt winded. And yet this was exactly what she'd asked for. Demanded. And when he bent his head to kiss her again, and started to open her shirt, she couldn't stop him because if she did he'd know that all of her proclamations were built on a very flimsy foundation.

With the lingering heat of their recent impassioned love-making still in her blood and heavy limbs, Alana's focus came back to the present. The earth below was an indistinct mass of brown mountains seen through breaks in the cloud. She sighed and let her head fall back against the seat, closing her eyes. She was playing with fire; she knew it. And all the trust issues in the world weren't going to keep her safe from harm.

As his private jet winged Alana home in style and comfort, the novelty and charmlessness of commercial travel was quickly reminding Pascal how far he'd come. Although, he could never forget his upbringing; it was branded onto his skin like a tattoo. He could remember how close he'd come to being one of the lost youths of the Parisian suburbs: lost to a life of crime and drugs, hopelessness. Until his mother had died and had thus saved him, by ensuring that he would go to live with his grandfather. She had redeemed herself and her woeful mothering by making sure he'd take another path, despite the fact that he'd been a representation of everything that had failed in her own life.

Pascal strode free of the gnarled mass of human traffic in Charles de Gaulle airport and sank into the back of his car which was waiting just outside the doors. Why was he thinking of such things now, when he hadn't thought of them in years?

Alana.

A woman was making him think of these things, when no other lover had ever done so. He had to concede that no other lover had taken him by the scruff of the neck and rattled him so completely. No other lover had evoked within him a compelling need to obey instinct over intellect. He hadn't lived like that for a long time. She connected to something within him, primitive and long-suppressed, deep and visceral. He searched desperately to justify this feeling, to rationalise it, but his brain wouldn't cooperate.

When she'd stood there earlier and had coolly informed him that she was fine with their temporary affair, that above all she didn't expect commitment, he should have been rejoicing. Wasn't it a man's ultimate fantasy? For a man like him, happy to take lovers for a short time until they bored him, or until they started looking for more.

Here he was, being offered this fantasy on a plate, and he well knew that she meant every word she'd said. It wasn't some kind of devious reverse-psychology. So why had he felt anything but relieved? Why had he wanted to challenge her? Why had that instinct not to let her go felt so strong? He'd certainly never aspired to the empty heights of marriage, either; he'd learnt at an early age that searching for that elusive happiness only bred disillusionment and pain. His parents had both proved in their own ways to be prime examples of that. His father had seen him as nothing but a threat to his own marriage, and had rejected him outright because of it.

Yet Alana was making him question the very bedrock on which he'd built his life. His sluggish brain finally kicked into gear: attraction. That had to be it. A rare form of lust. He just hadn't met a woman who'd taken possession of his body and mind before, that was all. That had to be all. OK, so she wasn't into anything permanent—well, neither was he. He just wasn't used to being on the receiving end of the ultimatum, that was all. He relaxed. Their affair certainly wasn't over yet. Not by a long shot.

'You know we're just concerned, love.'

'I know, Mam, I know.' Alana sank into her couch, still wearing her coat.

'He seems like a very nice man. He's awfully important, isn't he?'

Alana bit back a rueful smile. *'Nice'* hardly did him justice. 'Em, yes, he's quite important. But, Mother, don't go getting any ideas, now. It's nothing special.' *Liar.*

Her mother trilled a laugh down the phone. 'I might not quite understand these new relationships, but, love, I know how hard it was for you when Ryan died. It's OK to move on now, it's been long enough. No one would expect you to mourn for ever.'

Alana felt a wave of isolation come over her. Her parents had never really acknowledged the fact that she'd been divorcing Ryan; it had simply been too painful for them to admit that one of their children had failed in their marriage that way. So, when Ryan had died so tragically just before the divorce had come through, Alana had known that in some awful way, it had allowed her parents to believe in the myth of her fairy tale. Was it any wonder she hadn't been able to confide in them?

After a few more words they finished the conversation, and Alana was relieved that her mother hadn't mentioned Pascal again. She shook her head and then resolutely turned off her phone before she could get another acerbic call from her sister, Ailish, who would no doubt have seen the same gossip rags as her mother. She and Pascal were all over the press; the reporters had been waiting at Dublin airport. She knew she'd been naïve to think for a second that perhaps people wouldn't be interested.

Why did she have to go and meet someone who made her feel alive again, someone she couldn't resist? Someone in the public eye on a level that made Ryan O'Connor seem as if he'd been in the Z-list celebrity pile? It was as if she'd had a list of things to avoid and had blithely ignored each and every one of them. Alana just hoped that she could look at Pascal one day soon and not feel that burning desire rip through her entire body like a life-sustaining necessity.

# CHAPTER SIX

THREE heady, passion-filled weeks later, that day was eluding Alana spectacularly as she looked down from her position in the press box to the VIP area in Croke Park. Déjà vu washed over her as she caught Pascal's eye and made a face before turning her attention back to the game between Ireland v England. Her heart was singing, her breath was coming fast, and her blood was zinging through her veins. She put her intermittent feelings of nausea down to that see-sawing feeling and tried to forget that she'd been compelled to buy an over-the-counter pregnancy test that morning on her way to work after Pascal had said goodbye to her from her own modestly sized double bed.

She wouldn't think about her late period or the pregnancy test now. It couldn't be possible. And yet, a small voice niggled, *it could*. But in the years of her marriage to Ryan, while they'd still been sleeping together, she hadn't had one scare despite not having used contraception. It had been the source of some of their main problems, and, while Alana had got checked out and been told everything was fine, Ryan had refused, clearly unable to deal with the fear that it could be something on his side.

The match picked up in pace just then and Alana let it distract her. At the end, Pascal found her as the usual scramble started.

'I've agreed to go on the post-match analysis panel to give my opinion on how I think the tournament is going to go. They're doing it in the press centre here.'

'OK,' Alana said, feeling slightly breathless and hating herself for it. 'I've some interviews lined up, and then I've got to head back to the studio, so I'll see you later.'

He nodded and bent close to her ear for a moment. 'I want to kiss you so thoroughly that you're boneless in my arms, but I don't think you'd thank me for that in front of the entire press-box.'

Alana felt boneless already, and fought the rogue urge to let him do exactly that. She just shook her head swiftly, alternately disappointed and relieved when he stepped away with a cool look on his face.

His tall, powerful frame disappeared down through the seats, taking a little piece of her with him. She sighed. She was in so much trouble, and she was potentially in a whole lot more trouble too. The kind of trouble that Pascal Lévêque wouldn't thank her for. And yet… She placed a hand on her belly. Right at that moment she thought that, if she was pregnant, it was something she'd always have for herself. A baby, a child.

Just then the cameraman signalled that they were ready to go with the first interview, and Alana gathered up her stuff and hurried down to the pitch.

By the time they were onto the last interview with one of the Ireland players, Alana was feeling exhausted. She glanced up and her stomach contracted painfully when she saw who it was—Eoin Donohoe, one of her late husband's partners in crime. He was a huge, intimidating presence, one of the biggest players on the team. Like Ryan, he, too, was married, but that hadn't stopped his own hedonism. Waves of old mutual antipathy flowed between them as Alana prepared to ask the questions. Eoin smiled at her, but it held a nasty edge which she ignored.

They were almost done with the live interview when Eoin said quietly, 'So, we see that you're moving on with your life. Poor Ryan's barely cold in the grave.'

The air went very still around them. Alana fancied she could hear a pin drop. 'Excuse me?'

'Everyone knew you couldn't wait to get rid of him and suck him dry so you could move on, but you've got the best of both worlds now, don't you? You've got all of Ryan's money, and now you've got one of the richest men in the world eating out of your—'

'I beg your pardon, Eoin,' she cut in quickly, having no doubt he'd not stop at saying something unbelievably crude. 'My husband has been dead for a year and a half, and it's no business of yours and never has been what I do with my personal life.' The vitriol in Eoin's eyes made Alana quail inside, but something else was starting to rise up, too, something she'd held down for a long, long time—the truth.

Eoin continued with ugly menace in his voice and face. 'Except that it's your fault he died, your fault the Irish team never recovered from Ryan's death. If you hadn't thrown him out when he was so vulnerable—'

It came up from somewhere deep and reflexive. Alana laughed. She actually laughed. And it felt so good that she kept laughing. She knew it was verging on hysteria, but the truth had risen so far now that she couldn't help it coming out. She'd had enough of being the scapegoat for Ryan O'Connor.

She stepped forward and pushed a finger into Eoin's massive chest, emboldened by the fact that he looked distinctly nervous now at her reaction.

'Let's get a few things straight here and now, shall we?' She didn't wait for an answer; everything was forgotten as she was borne aloft on a wave of something like mad euphoria.

'My husband was a lying, cheating, womanising, gambling, pathetic excuse of a man. And I'm not the only one who knew it. My only sin was that I helped to perpetuate the myth, that I helped the world to see and believe in Saint Ryan. He made my life a misery. And *you* were part of that. I know all about you, too, Eoin Donohoe; don't you think people or even your wife would like to hear about your drunken, whoring binges in—'

'Shut up, you little bitch.'

His stark language, the threat in his tone and the way his face had twisted, made Alana step back in fright. Someone jumped in and physically restrained Eoin, he looked so angry.

The world came back into focus and Alana was stunned. Had she really just said all that? She looked around at the cameraman wildly. It wasn't Derek, it was a new guy, young and scared-looking. Derek would have had the sense to stop filming. Her stomach went into free fall.

She said through stiff, cold lips, 'Please tell me you stopped filming?'

He gulped and went puce, lowering the camera. 'I—'

Alana raised a shaky hand to her face; her other one was still wrapped around the microphone. 'Oh God.'

A low, threatening voice sounded near her ear, turning her blood cold. 'Well done, Cusack. You've done it now; you'd better be prepared for the fallout.'

She took down her hand and watched as Eoin sauntered away. He hadn't even tried to stitch her up. She'd done it all by herself. The minute he'd come out with his first provocative comment she should have wrapped up the interview and that would have been that. It was no worse than some of the barbed comments people had thrown at her since Ryan had died. Yet she'd never felt the need to defend herself till now.

In the temporary studio set up at the other end of the pitch for the after-match analysis, there was a deathly lull as the panel absorbed what had just happened. Luckily they had just cut to a commercial break, but the damage was done. Pascal's face was like granite.

When she finally let herself into her house later, Alana felt shell shocked, as if she'd been put through a wringer and left flat and limp on the other side. When she'd walked back into the newsroom, she'd been summoned immediately to Rory's office and had been fired on the spot. The entire slanging match had been aired on national television, in front of the country and in front of the panel of experts discussing the match. And Pascal. Apparently he'd held his tongue on air, but afterwards had voiced his concerns for the image of the tournament, and the image of his bank's involvement in the face of the rapidly escalating scandal. That was what Rory had told her as he'd all but flung her contract at her.

'I knew you were liable to be a problem when I hired you!'

'And yet,' Alana had pointed out in a desperate bid to try and save herself, 'I proved myself to be reliable, well informed, and you even told me last week that I was the one you trusted most to do the hard-hitting interviews.'

'Yes, Alana,' he'd replied wearily, sitting down behind his desk. 'But you brought your baggage with you, didn't you?'

She'd kept it together and had just said quietly, 'I guess I did.' Even from the grave her husband was having the last laugh.

As Alana sat on her couch now and thought of everything that had just happened she couldn't stop the nausea rising. She just made it to the bathroom in time and emptied the contents of her stomach. As she washed her face, she thought of something, and with a fatal air went back out to her bag and extracted the chemist's bag. She went back into her tiny bathroom.

The day couldn't get any worse.

And then it just did.

* * *

She tried to ignore the doorbell which was ringing persistently, the door-knocker banging violently. But the thought of her neighbours hearing the commotion finally made her move off her couch and out of the state of shock that had held her immobile for the past few minutes. She opened the door and didn't wait to see who it was. She knew.

Pascal came in and towered over her, the door shut behind him.

'What the hell was all that about?'

Alana moved around to her armchair and sat down, because she was afraid she might fall. 'That was me, finally airing my dirty laundry. In front of the nation, no less.'

Pascal had moved to the centre of the small sitting-room, and glared down at her. 'And in front of the entire Six Nations public too. I believe the news is hitting the airwaves as we speak. The hotel where the after-match party is being held has had to call for police assistance in dealing with the hordes of paparazzi already camped outside.'

Alana winced.

Pascal grunted something unintelligible and sat down on her couch. She was still a little too numb to react.

'So? Are you going to tell me what happened?'

Alana shrugged. She looked at him, but didn't really see him. 'He pushed me too far. For months people have been making snide comments about how I was so cruel to Ryan—how could I have thrown him out?—and the truth was exactly what I said.'

Pascal drove a hand through his hair. 'But it's crazy. The things you said—'

'Were all true.' Alana felt life-force coming back into her bones, the shock wearing off. This man and his concern for appearances was the reason she'd just lost her job, and the reality of what that meant was beginning to sink in.

She stood up and crossed her arms. 'I'm not really in the

mood to discuss this actually, would you mind leaving? I think you've done enough for one day.'

He stood, too, bristling. He pointed at his chest. '*Me?* I'm not the one that has just ripped the rose-tinted glasses from a nation of mourners. Whatever your husband might have been, Alana, surely there was a more decorous time and place to tell the truth?'

She stepped up to him, shaking. 'Do you really think I thought it through logically for one second Pascal—and then went ahead thinking it would all be OK?' She stepped back again, breathing heavily. 'Of course I didn't. It just came out. And in all honesty, I probably couldn't stop myself if it happened again. He provoked me.'

Pascal recalled what Eoin Donohoe had said, and recalled, too, his urge to go and lift Alana bodily out of his way so that he could shield her. He'd been genuinely concerned for her safety as he'd watched her confront the huge man. She'd looked so tiny and fragile, standing up to him. The protective instinct had caught him unawares as the events had unfolded in front of him, but then he'd also had to assess the potential damage as a barrage of calls had immediately jammed the phone lines in the studio.

Pascal couldn't keep the censure from his voice. 'He may have provoked you, but you've unleashed a storm now.'

He saw how Alana paled dramatically. But his own head was still ringing from the board of his bank wanting to know what on earth was going on, why a storm in a teacup was threatening to reduce the famous rugby-tournament to the level of a sideshow. And what it was already doing to their reputation on Europe's stock markets.

Alana felt a wave of weariness. 'It'll die down soon enough. It's not as if people are going to be faced with me, anyway; I've been sacked.'

Pascal's head reared back. '*Sacked?*'

She nodded and looked at him, hardening her heart and insides to the way he made her feel, even now. The weariness fled and anger rose, hot and swift. How could he be so cavalier about her life? Her independence was gone, everything she'd built up destroyed. 'Rory sacked me as soon as I got back. And as it was in part to do with your reaction, you needn't act so surprised.'

Pascal's face darkened ominously, features tight. 'I didn't know he'd done that.'

'Well, he did.' Her hands were clenched into fists at her sides.

'I would have never have advocated that you lose your job over this. To suggest that is ridiculous.'

His words rang with conviction, and he seemed affronted that she thought he would be so petty. She knew she couldn't blame him for the fact that Ireland was so small that the merest whiff of scandal could run for weeks and weeks and wreck a career overnight. The immediate future lay starkly ahead of her, especially with the brand-new knowledge that she held secret in her belly. The anger drained away and she felt weary again; it was too overwhelming to try and get her head around it. And at the centre of everything stood this man who was turning her upside down and inside out.

She sat down again when a wave of dizziness went through her. Immediately Pascal was at her side, bending down, a hand on her knee. She tried to flinch away, but he wouldn't release her.

'What's wrong?' he asked harshly.

'Nothing,' she answered quickly, restraining the urge to place a hand on her belly. Then hysteria rose again. 'Unless you count the fact that I'm now jobless and about to be homeless, too.'

'What are you talking about, Alana? You're not making sense.'

'Sense! If I had *sense* I wouldn't have opened my mouth

earlier.' She was already hoping he'd forget what she'd just said. But of course he didn't; his logical brain was sifting through everything.

'What do you mean, homeless?'

She wished he'd move back. He was crowding her, exactly as he'd done that first time they'd met and had been in the car on the way to the restaurant. She cursed her runaway mouth inwardly.

'What I mean is that, without a job, I'm going to be homeless. I have this month's mortgage paid, and after that... nothing.'

He stood up again and she looked up.

He was remote, more remote than she'd ever seen him. 'How is that possible? You must have been left a fortune.'

Alana felt his coolness touch her deep inside. She stood up, too, moving back towards her galley-kitchen as if seeking refuge. This was the first time she'd ever contemplated telling anyone the whole truth. She grimaced inwardly, apart from her recent exposé.

She shook her head. 'That's just it. It's a myth. Ryan gambled everything away with people like Eoin, on stupidly lavish expensive weekends to places like Las Vegas. They'd hire private jets, stay in the best hotels—drink, drugs, girls, gambling. They did it all. When Ryan died, he had debts to the tune of millions, and no one knew. He kept up the pretence all along. If we hadn't had the house to sell in Dalkey, I'd have had to declare myself bankrupt. Thanks to my own savings, which didn't amount to much, I was able to buy this house and set up a loan agreement with Ryan's debtors to pay the rest of the money back. Without my job, the repayments will fall behind immediately. This house is the least of my worries; the minute the repayments stop, they'll come after me.'

Alana didn't glean any comfort from Pascal's shocked

look. She knew well that on some level he'd still had her cast in the role of an ex-WAG—the derogatory term for the wives and girlfriends of sports stars. She couldn't blame him; she'd seen the way he'd look at her sometimes, as if waiting for her to trip herself up, reveal herself to be the silly bimbo that most of those girls were.

'I'll talk to Rory.'

Alana shook her head vehemently. 'No, that'll make things even worse. The last thing I need now is to be pushed to the forefront of everything again.'

'But maybe he can keep you behind the scenes for a while.'

'It wouldn't work.' She could just imagine the snide comments, the looks.

'What about your family? Don't they know about this?'

A spasm of pain clenched Alana's insides. She hated admitting this, knowing it would be hard to understand. 'No; they don't know. I was as guilty as Ryan for keeping up the pretence.' She avoided Pascal's eye. 'They just…they don't have the kind of resources I needed. They had their own things going on, and my parents are old, frail. They didn't need to hear about my problems.'

Pascal's tone was frigid. 'It sounds to me like it was a problem worth sharing.'

She looked at him, feeling defensive. 'It was my decision, OK? My family aren't that wealthy, my parents certainly aren't any more. They live comfortably, but they've earned that. I couldn't burden them with the mistake I made.'

'Is that how you saw your marriage?'

The way Pascal asked the question so softly made Alana feel even more vulnerable. She had to push him back; she knew well it was only a matter of time now before he ran as fast as he could from her car wreck of a life.

'For a long time, yes I did, which is why I'm determined not to make the same mistake twice.'

He started advancing towards her, and Alana backed away further.

'Is that what you see happening here—a mistake in the making?'

Alana shook her head, confused. Did he mean *them*? 'I don't... What are you talking about? This isn't anything like that.' *It's worlds apart.*

He was still advancing into her kitchen, making the space become tiny. Alana was starting to feel desperate. She felt so raw and vulnerable right now that if he so much as touched her... She stopped abruptly as her hand that had been sliding along the counter hit something. Instinctively, she covered it. She knew immediately what it was; she'd left it there in her shock and confusion just minutes before. Pascal's eyes darted to where her hand had made the betraying, concealing movement. Alana gulped as he looked back to her. She felt guilty. She looked guilty.

'What's that, Alana?'

'Nothing,' she said, almost hopefully.

'So why are you trying to hide it?'

'I'm not.'

'Show me what it is.'

'It's nothing, just rubbish.' Desperation tinged her voice, and in a rising surge of panic and rejection at the thought of confronting this, too, when so much had just happened, she whipped it off the counter top and whirled around to put it in the bin. But before she could a strong arm wrapped itself around her midriff and pulled her back into a hard body. With effortless strength, Pascal reached round and pulled the object from her hand. She closed her eyes. Their breathing sounded harsh in the small space, and she could imagine him trying to make sense of what he was looking at.

Alana could feel the tension come into Pascal's body. His arm grew even more rigid around her. She knew it wouldn't take long for him to make sense of it. These days pregnancy tests were idiot proof and the results immediate—the word *'pregnant'* wouldn't have taken a six-year-old long to figure out.

And then abruptly, so abruptly that she stumbled a little, Pascal released her. She turned round to look up but he wasn't looking at her, he was looking at the pregnancy test. After a long, tense moment he finally looked at her and she fought not to wince under his almost-black look.

'It's pretty self-explanatory.'

He nodded. 'Yes, crystal-clear.'

He turned and walked back into the sitting room, holding the test in his hand. Alana followed warily. He turned then, and she stopped in her tracks at the harsh lines on his face.

'And were you planning on keeping this little secret to yourself, too, shouldering this as another burden? Another mistake?'

Pain lanced her. 'I did the test just before you arrived. My period is late... I've been feeling a bit sick, so I bought it this morning on my way into work. Of course I would have told you.' *Eventually.*

'Oh, really?' His voice could have turned milk sour. 'I find that hard to believe, when you were about to throw it in the bin as nothing more than a piece of rubbish. Perhaps you've already decided what you want to do with our baby.'

*Our baby.*

The simple words of acknowledgement and acceptance rocked through Alana like an atom bomb. She put her hands instinctively on her still-flat belly. 'Of course I haven't decided anything, and certainly not what you seem to be implying. And I *was* going to tell you. It's just...I've barely had time to take it in myself. I think you can agree that today has packed more than its fair punch.'

Hating herself for feeling so weak as another wave of dizziness washed over her, she couldn't help swaying slightly. Words resounded in her head: *jobless, homeless, pregnant.* She'd really made a mess of things this time.

With a muttered curse Pascal was by her side and made her sit down on the couch.

'When was the last time you ate?'

Alana had to struggle to recall. Pascal cursed again colourfully. 'Don't tell me you haven't even eaten all day?'

He threw off his coat and went into her kitchen and started opening the fridge and looking on her open shelves. Feeling totally bemused and numb, Alana watched as he took out bread, butter, cheese, tomatoes and made a sandwich. He brought it back over on a plate and handed it to her, watching her until she'd eaten the whole thing, even though it was the size of a doorstep.

When she was done, he took the plate and set it aside, then he stood up and started to pace. He ran a hand through his dishevelled hair. He looked dishevelled all over, and Alana could feel her pulse stirring to life. His shirt was coming out of his trousers, the top button of his shirt undone. He rounded on her then, taking her by surprise. Her eyes had been on his bottom, and she coloured guiltily. How could she be thinking of that at a time like this?

But it seemed as if she was not the only one. Pascal dropped down onto the couch beside her, coming close, and before she could stop him he was undoing the top button of her shirt.

'That's better. I can't concentrate when you're all buttoned up.'

Alana backed away into the corner of the couch. Pascal's brows rose. 'It's a bit late for that, don't you think?'

She was beginning to feel stifled, threatened—sensory overload. She shimmied out from under him and stood up. Pascal sat back and looked up from under hooded lids. Alana's insides clenched.

'So when do you think it happened? I thought we were careful.'

'We were,' she said crisply, and then remembered the back of the car that night in Rome. Colour washed through her cheeks again. She looked down and caught his eye. She couldn't read his expression. But it seemed as if he could read her mind.

'Yes, there was that time. Or the bath afterwards.' Pascal had known well he was being careless, but for the first time in his life that concern had assumed secondary place to fulfilling his physical needs. And in the intervening days he hadn't even thought about it. More fool him. Yet, even more astounding to him right now was the equanimity he felt in the face of this news. In fact, what he was feeling was an inordinate sense of *rightness*. A sense of something his grandfather had passed onto him, something he'd never realised he possessed before: a sense of family.

Along with it came the memory of what it had been like to be shunned, rejected, and surging up within Pascal now was a zealous desire to give this child, *his* child, the kind of acknowledgement he'd never had. The revelation stunned him.

Alana started to pace, anything to avoid looking at him, wanting him. She had to sort her head out. She couldn't let him distract her.

'Look. This has happened. It was reckless and silly, but we both know where you stand on this kind of thing.'

He stood up and was immediately dangerous, towering over her. 'Oh, we do?'

Alana felt like stamping her foot childishly. 'Yes! I can't imagine you're happy to be faced with a pregnant—'

'Mistress?' he asked equably.

'I hate that word. I'm not your mistress.'

'Then what are you? Go on—say it, Alana.'

He was goading her, teasing her, even now. She glared up

at him, arms crossed. 'I'm your latest lover. The one in between your last one and your next one.'

His expression hardened, his eyes flashed. 'Yes. But now you're my pregnant lover, so that changes things somewhat.'

'Are you trying to tell me that you're seriously happy with this?'

'Not happy, exactly, no,' he bit out, feeling defensive. 'But how do you know that I haven't always wanted a child someday?'

'Have you?' she shot back.

Now Pascal was the one backing away, feeling a little poleaxed again. His recent revelation was too new, too raw to articulate. This whole afternoon was taking on an unreal hue, as if he'd stepped into some mad time-warp. He was in a tiny house in the middle of Dublin with a woman who'd stepped into his life and turned it upside down. She'd just told him she was pregnant, and he was still there. He wasn't running as fast as his legs could carry him away from her, which was how he'd always envisaged reacting to such a scenario.

He looked at her steadily and tried to ignore the way her hair was escaping the confines of its neat bun, the way he could see the hollow at the bottom of her throat where he'd opened the button. Even now, more than ever, he wanted her. He answered almost distractedly, 'Yes…of course I did. On some level.' *Someday.*

His mind cleared and fixed on Alana. 'What about you?'

He saw her hand go to her belly again; she'd done that a few times, almost as if to protect the unborn child from something—*their* unborn child. Something in his chest felt tight.

Alana turned away from Pascal's gaze for a moment. He was looking too deeply, seeing too much. When she turned around, his expression had lost that intensity; it was more innocuous.

'Yes. I always wanted children. We…myself and Ryan… tried, but nothing happened. And I was always grateful then that we hadn't. No child deserved to be born into our sham of a marriage.'

'And what will this be, Alana?'

She looked up into his eyes, panic trickling through her. He was so powerful, a million times more powerful than Ryan ever had been. He was cold, remote, and she had that prescience again of what it would be like to cross him—she wouldn't win.

'This will be just us, having a baby. I'm not going to marry you, Pascal.' She was shaking her head, moving away. He advanced.

'I wasn't aware that I'd asked you,' he said silkily.

She flushed. 'Well, isn't that…how you people operate?'

He threw back his head and laughed, but Alana knew he wasn't amused. 'What do you think I am, a masochist? Why would I want to marry a woman who doesn't want to marry me?'

*And who I don't want to marry*, he should have added. Alana shrugged, feeling silly now. 'So that you can have control over our baby. Child.'

He was very close now.

'Oh, I'll have control, Alana, as much as you do. We don't need to be married for that. It'll be my name on the birth certificate, and I expect to be involved every step of the way.'

'But…' Alana's throat was dry. 'But how is that going to work?'

Pascal's hand reached out and she felt his finger trail from her jaw down to her neck, to the hollow where her pulse beat fast and unevenly.

'It's simple—for now you'll come back and live in Paris with me. We can sort things out from there.'

# CHAPTER SEVEN

THREE days later Alana finally had to acknowledge that she really hadn't had a choice. Not that it made her feel any better. What could she have done? Her family was reeling from the revelations. The country was reeling. Reporters had camped out on her parents' front lawn until Pascal had hired security guards to protect them and drive the reporters away. She'd created an unholy row. She'd never confided in her brothers and sisters, so to seek help now—and in doing so bring the media circus behind her—would be unforgivable. The best thing she could do was to disappear. But unfortunately that could only happen with the one person she really didn't want to have to face: Pascal. By coming to Paris, she knew she'd tacitly agreed to stay for an indeterminate amount of time— till things calmed down at home, or until she could get another job. Either way, she was in no position to call the shots for now.

Yet she'd prevaricated, resisted, and watched with mounting horror as the story had taken hold in the press, had watched as her tiny house and square had come under siege. Pascal had finally battled through reporters the previous day, his face rigid with censure as he'd rounded on her once inside the tiny space.

'This is ridiculous. If you don't leave and come with me

right now, *today*, you're going to turn this into something even bigger. They know where you live, where your family lives. You'll have to leave the house at some stage, or were you planning on surviving on air and water?' His scathing glance had taken in the already bare-looking shelves in her kitchen.

Alana had never felt so undone, so threatened, in all her life. Even when Ryan had been at his worst, she'd had a level of freedom, space. He hadn't touched the part of her deep down that this man was trampling all over. She'd shaken her head as much in negation of that as anything else. 'Please. Don't make me; I can't leave. I'll manage somehow.'

'How?' he'd asked curtly. 'As of next month, you're facing repossession. You're hardly in a position to go out and seek employment within a two-hundred-mile radius of this country. I've stayed here out of concern for you and your family, but I have to return to France.' He'd gestured to the curtains drawn over her window. She could hear the jostle of people outside. 'Are you really ready to take them on by yourself?'

Alana had looked at him and let easy anger rise. She'd lashed out as much at herself as him, but made him the target. 'This is all your fault. If you hadn't pursued me, if you hadn't wanted me—'

Her words were cut off as he bridged the gap between them and gripped her upper arms, hauling her close. Words died in her throat as she felt her body come flush against his. She'd never seen him look so angry.

His mouth was a thin slash of displeasure. 'I wanted you, yes, but you acquiesced, Alana. I'm not the reason your marriage failed, and I'm not the reason you never spoke the truth before now, and I'm certainly not the reason you felt compelled to spill your guts the other day.'

Alana gulped as she looked up, held captive in his hands, her body already responding to his. The problem was, he *was* the reason, but she knew she couldn't blame him. He'd changed her; since the first moment their eyes had met, something in her had started to melt and breathe again. 'I'm sorry,' she said quietly, soberly. 'You're right. It's not your fault.'

'Damn right it's not my fault. If anyone is to blame, then it's you because *this*, the way you make me feel, is all your fault.'

He looked at her for a long, searing moment before hauling her even closer into his chest, and claimed her mouth with his. It was passionate, bruising, all-encompassing. Pascal's hands held her easily, pressing her close into his fast-burgeoning arousal. And she did nothing to stop him because she couldn't. Didn't want to. He hadn't touched her since it had all come out. And she needed this, wanted him so badly that nothing else mattered but him here, right now, with his mouth on hers, giving her life. Restoring sanity, while taking it away spectacularly.

He pulled back after a long, incendiary moment. They were both breathing fast, hearts thumping in unison. She looked up at him helplessly, aghast at how even now he had the power to render her speechless with just a kiss.

When he spoke, it made something cold descend into Alana's belly; his voice was so cool, so devoid of the passion she felt in his body. 'Have you also forgotten that you're carrying my child? And for that reason alone, if nothing else, you will be afforded my protection whether you like it or not. This isn't just about us any more, Alana.'

Now Alana stood at the window of Pascal's top-floor apartment near the Champs-Elysées in Paris, arms folded. The view over the Parisian rooftops was stunning, taking in the Arc de Triomphe in the distance. Where the apartment in Rome had had something homely about it, something Alana had instinctively preferred, this was sumptuous on another level. The antiques and priceless art, the luxurious curtains and ankle-deep carpets screamed decadence.

She sighed and turned to survey the room again. Despite

its objects, its gilded antique furniture, it felt empty somehow. They'd arrived yesterday evening. Pascal had overseen her pack her things in her house and had then escorted her through the crush in the square. In his car on the way to the airport she'd made her calls, explaining to her parents that she was going away for a while to let things die down. They had been understandably concerned, and to her surprise Pascal had taken the phone out of her hand and had reassured her father that she would be fine, giving him his phone numbers and also assuring them that their protection wouldn't be lifted until Pascal was sure they would be left in peace. His easy reassurance had made her hackles rise, but had also conversely alleviated her awful, burning guilt.

Pascal had shown her to a separate bedroom when they'd arrived, clearly having had no expectation that she would share with him, and Alana had to wonder now what her role would be. And why she felt so confused about that—about what she wanted. This was exacerbated by the fact that she'd barely seen him since then. After having showed her where everything was, pointing out some food ready-prepared for eating, he'd informed her that he had work to do and had disappeared into a study.

Then this morning, he'd been up and gone to work when she'd emerged from her room, feeling like a train wreck, even after an amazingly deep sleep. He'd left a note on the kitchen counter with a long list of numbers and assistants' names. His writing was as distinctive and boldly authoritative as him:

If you need anything, just call. I've set up an account in your name at my bank with funds, should you need anything. My assistant will be around shortly with bank cards. Please make yourself at home. I will be back late, so don't wait up. I'll be eating out.
Pascal.

And just like that, here she was—pregnant with Pascal Lévêque's child, at the centre of a storm of controversy at home and conveniently sidelined to…where, exactly?

'I've made an appointment with a gynaecologist near here for tomorrow morning. You need to start thinking about yourself and the baby.'

Alana bristled; as if she'd had time to think about anything else. She'd hardly seen Pascal, had walked what felt like the length and breadth of Paris on her own, and now he was ordering her around only minutes after coming in the apartment door at the end of a long, lonely week for her. She lashed out at his easy assumption that she was here for good. 'I'd prefer if I could choose my own doctor, thanks, and there are plenty of gynaecologists in Dublin.'

A muscle clenched in his jaw. Alana was trying to ignore the way he looked so sexy in his suit. Suddenly to be faced with him after days of not touching him was making her equilibrium very shaky. She had to wonder if she'd imagined that kiss in her house the day he'd taken her away. Was their affair, in fact, over for him? Had the pregnancy killed his desire?

'She's the best in Paris. And who said anything about having the baby in Dublin? You're here now, Alana.'

Her eyes clashed with his, and her hands clenched at her sides as she regarded him across the kitchen where she'd followed him when he'd arrived home. Now she regretted the puppy-dog-like impulse. And her insecurity. 'I don't believe we've actually discussed this, Pascal. I have every intention of having my baby at home. As far as I'm concerned, I'm just here until things die down.'

'You mean, *our* baby.'

'I mean, *my* baby. This is not a traditional relationship. I've no problem with you being involved, but I'm making the decisions to do with my body and how I want this to proceed.'

'The medical system here is one of the best in the world,' he declared arrogantly, and Alana opened her mouth but faltered. He was right.

'That may be so. But when this baby is born, I'm going to want the support of my family. Here I've no one.' Alana felt a rising sense of panic that Pascal would just keep her here, like some kind of animal in a zoo.

She had her hand on her belly again, in an unconscious gesture of protection. She was dressed down in jeans and a loose shirt, and Pascal could see the outline of her bra underneath, white and plain, and yet more seductive than the flimsiest lingerie he'd seen on her yet—the memory of which was all too vivid. His jaw ached from holding it so tight. His belly burned with a fire that only the woman in front of him could quench, and he knew that would only be momentary. One taste of her and he'd want more. Much more. His body thrummed with sexual hunger, but it was a hunger he feared would hurt her, it was so strong.

That was why he found himself in the novel position of holding himself back. His head was scrambled. Alana wasn't just his lover any more, she was the mother of his unborn child. That elevated her to a place he wasn't quite sure he knew how to navigate. He knew nothing about pregnant women. So he'd done what he thought was best, given her some space—himself, too, if he was honest. The knowledge of impending fatherhood was bringing up all sorts of long-unexplored emotions and memories, not least of which was this desire to nurture and protect. He'd buried himself deep in work to try and avoid being alone with her as much as possible. But his good intentions were feeling very elusive now as she stood in front of him with bare feet, hair down, looking as sexily undone as his most rampant fantasy. Not a scrap of artifice or make-up.

'You're telling me that you will expect the support of your family, when up until now you've had no problem shunning it?'

Alana blanched. How was it that he could see her coming from three-thousand miles away? And why had she felt compelled to tell him all about her family?

'You haven't even told your parents yet.'

He was remorseless, and Alana felt exposed. 'I'm not going to tell anyone until the three-month mark, when it's safer. Anything could happen between now and then. It's such early days, we might not… It might not even…'

Pascal negated her fears with a slashing movement of his hand, a quick, violent surge of something protective rising up within him. 'Don't even say that. You will be fine. This baby will be fine.' The strength of the emotion that gripped him made him feel a little shaky, even Alana had stepped back, her eyes growing huge.

'Look.' He forced a reasonable, steady tone into his voice, belying what was under the surface. 'You need to have an initial check-up appointment, admit to that at least?'

Alana forced herself to take a deep breath. She was feeling overwhelmed, all at sea, itchy under the surface of her skin, unbelievably vulnerable and…homesick. The sting of tears burnt the back of her eyes, and a lump lodged in her throat. To her utter horror and chagrin, she saw Pascal's eyes narrow on her face. He came closer, and she feared even moving in case she shattered and fell apart.

'What is it, Alana? What's wrong? You seem…edgy.'

She could have laughed out loud if she'd had the wherewithal—*edgy?* She'd been on a knife-edge ever since she'd laid eyes on this man. He was standing so close she could smell him. She shook her head faintly and tried to control her emotions.

He came closer and the air seemed to swirl headily around them. It was the bizarrest sensation; the closer he came to her, the better she felt, the less isolated, the less lonely. But also the more confused.

'Alana, I can see *something* in those expressive eyes of yours.'

She tried to step back, but her legs wouldn't move. She threw out a hand as if to gesture around them. 'What on earth could be wrong, Pascal? Within a week I lost my job, found out I was pregnant, have moved homes and now I just... I've been alone all week, and it's just...' This time she couldn't stop them. The dam she'd been holding back burst and tears fell, hot and thick, down her face; her throat worked convulsively.

Through her blurred vision Pascal loomed large, and then Alana felt herself being enfolded in his arms, and held so tenderly and carefully against his chest that it made her cry even harder. And this wasn't pretty, silent crying, this was loud, snotty, shuddering, gasping crying. For what seemed like an age. And as she cried Alana realised that she'd never cried once in all the years of her marriage, even at the end. Even at Ryan's funeral. She'd locked her pain deep inside and it felt like it was all pouring out now, along with all her fears for the future and for her baby. *Their* baby.

Without her knowing how he did it, Pascal had taken Alana into the sitting room and she found herself sitting on a couch, still cradled against his chest. When her crying finally began to stop and became deep, shuddering breaths, she pulled away a little. His shirt was soaked.

'I'm sorry.' She couldn't look at him, and tried ineffectually to wipe at her damp face, which she could well imagine was not a pretty sight. Her eyes felt sore. He pulled a handkerchief from his pocket and handed it to her. She took it and blew her nose loudly, moving away from him. She was mortified. She'd never cried like that, even in front of her own mother.

He moved away for a second and came back. She saw a glass with dark liquid appear in front of her face. She looked at him swiftly. 'I don't think I should…' He made a very Gallic facial expression. 'I'm sure a small sip won't do any harm.' So she took a tiny sip. She could feel reaction start to set in, her legs and hands start to shake, and was glad of the burning sensation of the liquid as it entered her stomach and its comforting warmth spread outwards. She put down the glass carefully.

'I'm sorry. I don't know where that came from.' Alana felt her hands taken in Pascal's and he pulled her gently round to face him. His face was cast slightly in the shadows of the softly lit room.

'No, I'm the one who is sorry. I shouldn't have left you alone all week.'

She felt something flutter in her chest, and Alana immediately wanted to scotch his obvious suspicion that she might have missed him. Or that she needed reassurance, like some wilting heroine or, God forbid, a lover who was falling in love with him. 'Don't be silly, you were busy. I understand that.'

His mouth tightened momentarily. 'I created more work for myself to avoid being alone with you.'

A severe pain lanced Alana. She shouldn't be feeling pain, yet she also couldn't quite believe he was being so harsh. So this is what it would feel like when the time came. Well, the time had come. She tried to pull her hands from his. He wouldn't let her go. A spark of anger restored her equilibrium. 'Pascal—'

'Let me explain. I don't think you know what I mean.'

Oh God, he was going to explain, and she'd just blubbered all over him. She spoke quickly, 'No, really, I do; it's fine.'

'Alana, *tais-toi!*'

Pascal's exasperation was palpable. She shut up.

'I've avoided being alone with you, because if we're in any kind of close proximity for more than two minutes, I want to take you to bed with an urgency that is not necessarily good for someone in your condition.'

Her *condition*. For a second Alana didn't even know what he meant. Her heart was thumping, and a treacherous surge of joy in her chest was threatening to strangle her. He did still desire her. But then at the intent, serious look on his face her mind and vision cleared. He was worried that he'd hurt her?

That all-too-familiar melting sensation was spreading through her chest, warming her like the brandy. 'Oh.'

'Yes. Oh.'

Alana tried valiantly not to let the desperation she felt sound in her voice. She knew it was there, though, when she stumbled over the words. 'Well...I don't think— That is, as far as I know, it's OK. I mean, lots of people don't even know they're pregnant at this stage.'

Her face was getting warm. Could he see how badly she wanted him? She prayed not.

'How are you feeling now?'

*Like I want you to rip my clothes off and make love to me right here:* the words resounded in Alana's head. She gulped and could feel a trickle of sweat roll down between her breasts. 'Fine. Absolutely fine. I haven't been sick once this week. So, unless it comes back...'

Pascal stood up and paced. Immediately Alana wanted him back by her side. 'You see, that's what I mean, you need to go and speak to the doctor so we know what to expect.'

He looked down at her with a stern expression, all hunger and desire erased from his gaze and eyes. Alana felt as if she was a dog in heat, and struggled to control her libido. Was this a side-effect of the pregnancy—like the way her breasts

felt so heavy and tender? If so, how was she going to cope
with the next eight months?

'So, we're agreed, we'll go to see the doctor tomorrow?'

Alana just nodded, only half-taking in what he was saying.
Her whole being was focused on the fact that he still desired
her and had been holding back.

He came back and sat down beside her. Alana tried not to
let the hunger she felt show on her face.

'Look, Alana, you need me now. Let me take care of
you...and the baby. Ireland is not somewhere you can go
back to anytime soon. Let things calm down. In the meantime,
let's just concentrate on the baby and preparing for that...'

He made it sound so easy. And, while Alana felt it was
important to assert her independence, she knew he was right.
For now. It wasn't just about the two of them any more.
She'd worry about the shifting parameters of their affair
later. The knowledge that he still desired her was intoxicating, she went to bed that night and slept properly for the first
time all week.

'The doctor said it's OK.'

Alana immediately winced and froze inwardly at how
baldly she'd let the words come out. She'd had no intention
of even saying anything, but standing here, back in the apartment, holding all the bumph from the doctor's office and the
baby books Pascal had insisted on buying, something primal
was rising up within her—a need that had to be acknowledged. Pascal turned to face her. He was dressed in faded
denims and a dark coat, cheeks slightly reddened from the
brisk breeze outside. Alana's heart clenched. She'd never
grow tired of looking at him.

He walked towards her, a glint in his eye. 'What's OK?'

Alana flushed but looked at him steadily, not backing
down. 'If we...you know...wanted to—'

'Make love?' he asked innocently, that glint looking decidedly suspicious.

'Yes,' Alana bit out through a clenched jaw, and wished that she didn't feel the way she did—that she wasn't enslaved by this man and his body and how he could make her feel. The doctor had pointed out that it was entirely natural to be feeling more desirous at the moment, the result of hormones. But Alana knew well that the pregnancy was only heightening what was already there in raw form.

Pascal came very close and took Alana's jaw in his hand, its delicacy testing all of his powers of restraint. His thumb smoothed the satin-soft skin of her cheek. He saw her pupils dilate and it had a direct effect on his body.

'We'll go for dinner later.' He had to put some kind of control on this wanton craving he had. She was *pregnant*, for God's sake.

Her jaw moved against his hand and he hardened, his erection straining painfully against the constricting material of his jeans.

'OK. Where?'

'You choose. I have to go to the office to pick up some papers; I'll be back in an hour.'

'You've booked us a table where?'

Alana looked at the guide book again, slightly mystified by Pascal's incredulous reaction. 'A restaurant called Lapérouse.'

His face looked slightly pained. 'Are you doing this on purpose?'

Alana was nonplussed. 'On purpose—why? It just sounds nice. It's one of the oldest restaurants in Paris.' She held out the book for him to see.

Pascal took the book and put it down. 'I know the restaurant—or, should I say, I know what it's famous for.' Then he took her hand to lead her out of the apartment and Alana followed.

'What do you mean "famous for"? Because Émile Zola and Victor Hugo used to go there?'

'Something like that,' he muttered. 'You'll see.'

It was now late evening. Pascal had been held up at the office, and the sky in Paris was darkening to an inky blue, stars popping out. She'd changed into a simple black dress. Pascal had showered and changed into dark trousers and a dark sweater under his black overcoat.

Alana shivered slightly despite her big padded coat when they got outside. Pascal went to flag down a cab, but she wasn't shivering from the cold; it was a shiver of anticipation. Because ever since this morning, and her brief, excruciatingly naked declaration that it was OK to have sex, something heavy and tangible had been humming between them. Alana was confused as to how things were going to go in general with this relationship, but one thing she knew for sure was this: Pascal's desire for her was finite, and soon—as soon as the pregnancy started to progress in earnest, she guessed— he'd be moving on. She just didn't know where that would leave her. Oh, she wasn't so silly to have fallen for him. Even now she could say with pride that she'd protected her heart. But…

'Here we go.'

Pascal was helping Alana into the back of a warm cab, stopping her train of thought. And then, with him so close to her on the backseat, his fingers tangled in hers, she was finding it hard to think any more.

They got out of the cab in front of an ornately decorated restaurant situated on the corner of a street, right on the banks of the Seine. It had old murals of lavishly dressed women on the panels outside, windows full of ancient books, bottles and delicate filigree balcony-railings around the first-floor windows.

'This is gorgeous,' breathed Alana as she looked up.

Pascal just grunted something unintelligible in reply. When they went inside and Pascal gave Alana's name, as she had made the booking, she saw him exchange a few words with the head waiter. The man looked at her curiously and smiled, leading them up through the main part of the dining room and then off to the side and to a door. There were rooms off to all sides, creating a warren-like ambience of hidden nooks and crannies.

Pascal looked at her with an indecipherable expression on his face as the waiter opened the door and indicated for her to step in. When she did, her heart stopped, and then started again with slow, heavy beats. It was a tiny, private dining-room, more like a salon, with a table set for two, a mirror along one wall and a banquette seat at the back on which sat plump, inviting velvet cushions. The colours were dark and earthy, unbelievably sensual. It was like a *boudoir*.

Alana heard the door click shut and turned to face Pascal, her face flaming.

'I had no idea this was here.'

His mouth quirked, his eyes glittering in the soft light. 'I believe you.'

Alana was very aware of the look in his eye, the lines of tension on his face. No wonder he'd reacted the way he had. She'd led them to a veritable seduction scene straight out of a fantasy. She walked further into the intimate space. 'What *is* this place?'

She could sense him close behind her and her body trembled.

'It's where the wealthy could dine privately in peace and seclusion, and also, it's said, where clandestine affairs took place. Look here.'

He directed her attention to crude scrapings on the mirror. 'This is where the women would test the diamonds they'd been given by their lovers to see if they were real or fake. Where they would write love messages.'

Alana leant close but couldn't make out what the faint, scrawled writing said. She was very aware of the space, their breathing, *them*. A discreet cough sounded outside the door, and Pascal opened it to let the waiter back in with menus and water. He took their coats and left again. Pascal indicated for Alana to sit down. They were practically side by side at the table. The banquette seat loomed large in Alana's imagination just behind them.

Pascal sat back easily, his huge body taking up most of the space, and drawled softly, 'Good choice.'

Alana felt prim. 'You know very well I had no idea about this.'

He sat up then and captured her hands, coming close. 'I know, I'm only teasing. The table you'd booked was in the main part of the restaurant, quite innocuous. *I* asked for one of these rooms.'

'You did?' she all but squeaked.

He nodded. 'I've heard about this place, but never been. It's been something of a fantasy of mine to see what it was like.'

'It is?' Alana was barely breathing now; her whole body was igniting and melting. She'd all but forgotten that they were even in a restaurant. The thought of inadvertently fulfilling one of Pascal's fantasies was so heady, so...

A discreet cough came from outside again, and Pascal let her hands go and called, *'Entrez.'* But his eyes barely left hers or her face as the waiter took their food order.

Alana wasn't entirely sure how or what she ate during that meal. The whole experience in that small space became about the senses. It felt as though she and Pascal had been removed from the world and set adrift in this little cocoon of sensuality and decadence. She knew courses came: Dublin Bay prawns to start, amazingly enough, and a ham dish as a main course, and then a wickedly dark chocolate-praline sorbet. Or she could have been completely wrong, because she knew she wouldn't be able to recall what they'd had if asked. The things she would be able to describe in detail had more to do with Pascal's gestures, the way his eyes crinkled appealingly when he smiled or laughed, the way he made her feel so hot inside.

A waiter had cleared the plates and was leaving small cups of coffee with an after-dinner liqueur for Pascal. He was almost at the door when Pascal issued a few rapid words in French. The waiter inclined his head, and when he'd left, Alana asked, 'What did you say to him?'

Pascal looked at her with a heavy-lidded gaze. 'I said that we would call if we needed anything else.'

He came close and his arm brushed across her breasts, making her breath stop as he drew her attention to a cord descending from the wall beside her. She hadn't even noticed it. 'We won't be disturbed again unless we pull that.'

Alana looked from the cord to Pascal; he didn't move back. His scent wrapped around her like a cloak of heavy desire. The sheer sexiness of him, and the room, overwhelmed her, and she lifted a hand to run her fingers through his hair, feeling the beautiful shape of his strong skull. And then, unable to wait any longer, the promise of fulfilment so close, she pulled his head to hers and their mouths touched.

A week of not touching blew up around them instantly. It could have been a lifetime, the way things escalated so rapidly. Without breaking contact, Pascal lifted Alana from her seat and moved them over to the lush banquette behind them. He took his mouth from hers and she followed him momentarily, as if loath to break even that point of touch. He laid her back against the huge cushions, gently, reverently.

He shrugged off his sweater, revealing a dark shirt underneath, and Alana watched with heavy-lidded eyes as he smoothed a hand down one of her thighs. She arched her back even at that chaste touch; every part of her seemed to be so sensitive, tingling. She wore thigh-high black socks and zip-up leather ankle-boots; she felt Pascal bend down and slip them off her feet before his hand travelled back up one leg, right up to where the sock ended and her flesh screamed for his touch. He smoothed that hand further up her thigh, causing her dress to ride up, and when his hand reached where her panties covered the moistening apex of her thighs, she stopped him.

Desperate need tinged her voice even as she said, 'We can't, not here. They could walk in.'

Pascal just shook his head. *'Non;* they know better.'

Alana's head sank back. Pascal's hand was covering her now, moving back and forth; she was helpless not to push herself into him, wanting more. He bent over her and kissed her deeply, before she felt air whisper over her skin and she realised that he was undoing the buttons at the front of her dress. With one hand, he pushed the sides apart to reveal her breasts, covered in blood-red lace.

'So beautiful…' he breathed, before gently pulling the lace of one cup down and rubbing a thumb back and forward over one tight tip. Alana bit her lip. Her breast was almost painfully sensitive; her body felt as though it was on fire. Pascal lifted one of her legs and brought it up and over so that it was bent on the seat beside him, opening her up to him even more. His hand still moved between her legs, and she could feel herself plumping, ripening, getting ready.

With her legs spread, Pascal moved even closer, and Alana finally found some autonomy of movement and stretched out her hands to open his shirt. Her fingers shook, and she could feel sweat break out on her brow. She needed that contact so badly, his naked chest against hers.

When his shirt was finally open, he bent again to take her

mouth. His hand had pulled down the sliver of lace covering her other breast, and to feel him like this was heaven. Alana moaned deep in her throat when his mouth moved away, and at the same time as his hand stopped teasing her and his fingers slipped in behind her panties to seek the passage to the wet hot heart of her, his mouth and tongue closed over one nipple, pulling it into his mouth and suckling fiercely.

Alana cried out; she couldn't help it. Although she bit back the next cry, her hands were speared in his hair, wanting to make him stop the torturous pleasure he was inflicting on her breasts, and also never wanting him to stop. Her hips bucked towards his hand. He was wringing every ounce of her being out in a never-ending stream of pleasure, but the pinnacle was elusive. It wasn't enough.

She managed to pull his head from her breast and looked up into dark, glittering eyes. She felt wild and wanton. 'I need more, I need *you*.'

'Alana,' he groaned softly, his own body throbbing so painfully that it genuinely hurt. 'I've no intention of taking you here; I just wanted to kiss you.'

'And see where that gets us? You said they wouldn't disturb us.' A part of her couldn't believe she was being like this. Talking like this. Demanding this.

Pascal looked into her green eyes that were darkened with desire, pupils so large and dilated that it was simply too much not to give into temptation. But, even so, he was not comfortable with this base part of him, a part of him that reminded him of other times he'd left behind. He'd done so much to be civilised, sophisticated. And yet patently there was still something untamed within him, something he'd already realised this woman tapped into effortlessly.

With a sense of futile inevitability, Pascal pulled down Alana's pants, slipping them off one leg. Pressing kisses to the fragrant inner skin of her thigh, he opened his own

trousers, pushing down constricting underclothes. He ma-
noeuvred them so that, while she was still reclined on the seat,
her legs were around his waist, and he leant over her. 'You're
sure about this?' As if he could turn back!

Alana could feel the heat of his erection as it pulsed near
her body. The heady, musky scent of arousal permeated the
air. She felt exactly like one of the courtesans from long ago.

She nodded. This was where her universe began and
ended.

That was all he needed. He couldn't turn away from this.
Shifting his hips forward slightly, he entered her with one
smooth thrust, all the way, burying himself so deep that he saw
her head fling back, muscles corded in her neck. Her arms
gripped his biceps. Her breasts were like lush fruits framed by
red lace.

He bent his head and paid homage to each hard peak, rolling and suckling them against his tongue. He could feel her
hips twitch and buck towards him, drawing him down and in,
holding him tightly before releasing him again. When he
looked up, she was looking right at him. It hit him straight
between the eyes, and he almost lost control there and then.

She was on the edge. He felt the delicious tension coil
through her body. A darker flush stained her dewed cheeks,
and then he felt the growing ripples of her release start around
his shaft as he drove in and out. And then he came, too, his
body thrusting rapidly until he had nothing left to give. It had
been fast and furious. In the aftermath, he rested on one
elbow, shielding her from his weight. He still lay within her,
and could feel the after-tremors of her body.

When he could, he moved back and then scooped her up
against his chest where she curled up into him. He sat like that
with Alana curled into his body for a long moment. Sweat
glistened on their skin. He could feel her soft breasts move
against him with her breath, and unbelievably he could feel

himself stir again. She felt it, too, and wriggled a little. Pascal gritted his teeth and jaw. As much as he wanted this to be an oasis, to take her again and again, he had to remove her from here. Again he felt that untamed part of himself emerge, and he really wasn't comfortable with that. It made him forget about being in control. And what was compounding this feeling now was the fact that Alana wasn't just a lover any more, she was the mother of his child. And, he had to acknowledge uncomfortably, even that knowledge didn't seem to diminish his impulses around her.

As Pascal held her cradled against him for those moments, heart rates returning to normal, a vision of the future opened up before him, the clarity of which stunned him. In an instant he realised that the image, the desire forming in his head, was something he hadn't been able to articulate before now, it had simply been too alien to him. He never would have imagined that he would feel this way about it. That he wanted it so badly he could taste it. The chaotic tumult of emotions and desires whirling through him became secondary as he finally saw the way to reconcile the way she made him feel, to put order on things. He tried to make sense of what had just happened. He had to pull back. He had to exert some control. Everything had just changed irrevocably.

In the taxi on the way home Alana was wrapped in a delicious haze of satiety. She still couldn't quite believe what had happened in a *restaurant*, albeit a private room, and she couldn't stop looking at Pascal. She lifted a hand to smooth the unruly tendrils of hair on the neck of his shirt. He caught her hand, lifted it to his mouth and kissed her palm. She felt like a different person, and a deep fear-inducing moment of panic gripped her. Was it already too late? Had she already allowed him in so far that she wouldn't be sane again? Would walking away from him, which would inevitably happen, destroy her?

All she knew was that even when she'd believed she loved her husband it had never felt like this, and she had a sick feeling that she couldn't keep pinning these feelings on sex.

Pascal was kissing her hand and looking into her eyes, but she felt a distance there. She'd felt it in the room after they'd made love. He'd been considerate and even tender, helping her to dress again. But there'd been a coolness there. As if he'd been embarrassed. By her wanton behaviour? She cringed inwardly even as he still captured her hand. And she wondered how she'd come to read him so well that she knew something had changed.

# CHAPTER EIGHT

SOMETHING was definitely wrong. Since that night in the restaurant a week ago, Pascal hadn't made another move to touch her.

Yet he hadn't left her alone like he had the first week. He'd come home early every day, they'd cooked or eaten out, but with an impregnable wall growing between them. Alana was too nonplussed and unsure to ask what was wrong. But all the time she was burning up inside, aching with desire, aching for Pascal to just reach out and touch her, kiss her. She wanted to make the move, but she was too scared of what his reaction might be, and she couldn't help but be afraid that this was the start of the end of his attraction for her. There had been something finite about the way he'd made love to her the other night.

All he seemed to want to do now was talk. About everything.

'Have you thought any more about what you want to do?'

Alana's attention came back to the present and the discreetly exclusive restaurant that Pascal had taken her to, which was round the corner from his apartment. She looked across the table at him and tried to bury the spike of lust that clenched her insides whenever their eyes met.

'I'm going to enrol in French classes to improve my

French. And I wouldn't mind looking for a job at some stage. I know there are English-language TV and radio stations here; they might be looking for temporary sports presenters.'

He inclined his head. 'I'll check it out, too, and I'm sure there's information on the Internet about job opportunities. I've told you, you're more than welcome to use my study whenever you want.'

Alana nodded. 'Yes, thank you.' She was a little bemused at how easily he was giving her autonomy; she wasn't sure what she had expected. She must have looked a little shocked, because Pascal sat back with a wry look on his face. 'What did you expect—for me to refuse you the chance to take up employment again? To become independent?'

She thought of the irony behind his words—she'd never been less independent. Alana flushed and said tightly, 'I appreciate you paying off Ryan's debts and looking after my mortgage while I'm here, but it just means that now I have to pay you back.'

The ease with which he'd sorted out her tangled finances had rankled with her. But she hadn't been in any position to fight him.

He sat forward now and she sensed the waves of tension coming off him. His voice was clipped, accent more pronounced. 'You know very well those debts were a drop in the ocean for me, and you're the mother of my child. I was careless in protecting you from getting pregnant. I was instrumental in you losing your job. It's the least I could have done. So please, don't mention it again, and I do *not* expect you to pay me back.' He was genuinely angry.

She cradled her coffee cup in her hand and forced herself to meet his gaze. 'I was careless in protecting myself, too, Pascal, it wasn't just your responsibility. I don't want to seem ungrateful, but we both know we're not exactly talking about a loan of a few-hundred euros here.' She shrugged and looked away for a second. 'It's just…Ryan didn't want me to work, even though I'd done a degree in media studies. I can't help but think that if I'd worked during my marriage, our finances wouldn't have been in such dire straits. When he died, I was allowed to become independent for the first time, and I vowed never to have to depend on anyone again.'

Pascal sat back slightly, grimly. 'Which is why you never confided in anyone and why you fought so hard to get a job, no doubt.'

Alana looked at him quickly. 'How did you know that?'

'Rory Hogan told me.'

Alana's mouth tightened. 'When he also told you about my marriage?'

Pascal nodded.

'Why did you marry him, Alana? Surely you could see what he was like?'

Alana shrank back. She really didn't want to talk about this—it was too deep, too personal, still too raw—and especially with this man so close. So she glossed over it as best she could, avoiding Pascal's eye. She knew she sounded clipped, tense. 'I married him because I loved him, of course.' If she could fool herself, maybe she could fool Pascal. 'We met at a function that was celebrating my Dad's career playing rugby, and he just came up to me and started talking.' She smiled then; this bit she didn't have to fake. 'He had what we call at home "the gift of the gab".' She sobered again. He'd made her believe in the dream, that marriage was for her. His gift of the gab hadn't lasted long. But by then it had been too late.

'Somehow I don't think you're telling me everything, Alana, but don't worry; one day you will.'

Alana looked at him swiftly. His gaze was penetrating, incisive, too knowing, and too much—alluding to a future that stretched ahead which she knew couldn't exist. She lashed out to take that intensity off her and her choices.

'What about you, Pascal? Why haven't you been snapped up by now? I'm sure some of the women you know aren't beyond asking you to marry them.'

Her use of the present tense, and dispassionate tone—as if she didn't care that he hadn't married before now—irritated Pascal intensely, and he fought against it, saying coldly, 'I never let any get that far.'

Or that close? Alana had to wonder. She shivered a little at the way he'd suddenly closed up, and could see what countless other women must have been faced with once the desire was on the wane. The only difference with her was that she was pregnant with his child.

He shrugged then, and surprised her by elaborating, 'We're not so dissimilar, you and I. My upbringing, with a single mother bent on finding an elusive state of happiness through marriage, has taught me never to view it with rose-tinted glasses.'

Alana was stunned into silence. 'What do you mean? Why did she want to get married so badly?'

His eyes seemed to bore into hers. 'My father was a married man from her home town that she had an affair with when she was eighteen. He told her he was going to leave his wife and children and marry her, but he never did. She moved to Paris in disgrace to have me, and made it her life's mission to find another man to marry. But no one wanted to take on a single mother and demanding child.

'When I went to live with my grandfather, my father was still in the village; he'd never moved away. He knew exactly who I was. I'd pass him in the street perhaps twice a day and he'd look through me as if I didn't exist. Then he'd go home and play happy families with his wife and my three half-brothers and sisters. *That's* why I never wanted to get married. If it can induce a man to turn his back on his own child, if it can induce a man to make a mockery of his vows…'

Alana's heart ached. She wanted to reach out and touch him but held back. She just said gently, 'You would never do that, Pascal. And there are plenty of people out there who have kids and manage to meet someone new; it's just unfortunate that your mother didn't. She must have been very lonely.'

Pascal felt a jolt in his abdomen at Alana's immediate assertion that he wouldn't do what his father had done; again that hitherto-unacknowledged sense of family that his grandfather had instilled in him rose up, shocking him anew. For a second Pascal forgot everything. Alana was getting close, seeing too deeply; it made him want to draw back, protect himself.

He knew he sounded curt. 'My mother blamed me for her pain and loneliness. But it got her in the end; she died of cancer when I was fourteen.'

Alana shook her head. 'I'm sorry. No matter how difficult your relationship was, she was your mother. That was when you moved down to your grandfather?'

He nodded abruptly, still feeling raw, exposed.

She thought of something then, something that had been niggling at her on and off. She leant forward. 'What's the connection between you and your grandfather and rugby? There's something there that you're not talking about.'

His eyes went flinty, exactly as they had that day in the interview. Alana had an impression of him feeling cornered. 'Are you asking now as the reporter? Hoping to get a scoop for your first piece from France?'

Alana straightened up, unbelievably hurt that he would think that after everything he'd just told her. 'Of course not.'

Their eyes were locked, brown and green. But Alana refused to back down and then she saw Pascal's eyes change, become less hard, his face softened. He reached out a hand and captured hers, and held it when she would have pulled away. The contact was making her blood race through her veins.

'I'm sorry. That wasn't fair. I know you're not like that.'
He'd looked down at their hands, and now he looked back up,
stopping her breath. 'The truth is, you speak of a subject that
is…very personal, something I've never discussed with anyone.'

Alana was utterly consumed by him at that moment; nothing else existed around them. Unbeknownst to them a waiter
was trying to get their attention, but gave up and walked
away.

'I'm sorry, I don't mean to pry. If it's that hard to talk…'

'No,' he said quickly, his hand tightening on hers. His eyes
locked onto hers. The sympathy he saw in their depths reminded him of what he wanted, what he'd vowed to set out
to achieve after that cataclysmic night in the restaurant. If he
wanted that, then he had to tell her everything. 'It's not that.
I can take you somewhere tomorrow, if you like. Perhaps it'll
be easier to explain then.'

She just nodded, every part of her warming under his gaze,
but then conversely she also felt like running as fast as she
could in the other direction. There was something about this
moment, this conversation. It was inviting a deeper intimacy
into their already ambiguous relationship, and yet that cool
distance was still there, confusing her. Alana's well-worn
alarm bells were coming back to clanging life.

The next day Alana's nerves were jangling. She could remember coming back to the apartment the previous evening,
how badly she'd longed for Pascal to make love to her so she
didn't have to contemplate all the mounting confusion,
worries and fears in her mind. Fears that were incoherent and
tantalisingly out of reach. Pascal had been preoccupied and
distant again. He'd merely said goodnight and shut himself
in his study.

Then he'd reminded her that morning that he wanted to

show her something. 'Don't you have work?' she'd asked
over the rim of her tea cup, trying not to let her eyes wander
down over his jeans-clad legs and his dark sweater. He'd just
shaken his head.

So now Alana was waiting outside the apartment for him
to bring his car round. When he appeared and pulled into the
kerb in front of her, her jaw dropped.

He got out and looked at her over the hood of the car.
'What is it?'

'This isn't your car.'

Amusement laced his voice, but something very panicky
was taking off in Alana's belly.

'I have a lot of cars. But you're right; this is a new one.'

'But…you had a sports car.'

'You said you hated those cars. You said they represented
inadequacy, and the inability of men to function sexually and
in the world.'

'I know I did.' Alana felt like wailing, remembering that
it had been a laughable argument to throw at him. But right
now she would have given anything to see his Porsche. She
actually felt slightly as if she were going to hyperventilate.
Or get sick.

'But this…this is…' She looked at him helplessly.

He quirked a brow in her direction and she was transfixed
by his eyes. 'A family car?'

That was exactly what it was. She tore her eyes away from
his. It was a sleek, brand-new, beautiful top-of-the-range
Mercedes family car.

When he came round and held the passenger door open for
her, she was too scared to look in the back and see if he'd actually bought a baby seat too. Panic gripped her like a suffo-
cating vice around her heart. He got in beside her and pulled
out from the kerb, and she could feel him send her a quick
glance.

'Are you OK? Are you feeling sick?'

Alana alternately shook her head and nodded; she didn't know *what* was going on with her. When he went to slow the car for a second, as if to stop, she put a hand on his arm, and even that brief touch sent a whole host of other feelings and sensations through her body. She jerked her hand away.

'No, I'm fine. Really.' She was a mess.

He flicked her another sideways glance as if to make sure and then said, 'I got the car for you. You'll need something. But I know the traffic in Paris can be daunting, so you can get used to it with me driving first.'

Alana's stomach stopped churning as if a switch had been flicked. It was the most bizarre and curiously deflating sensation. Of course; silly her. He didn't mean that the car was for *them*. He wasn't buying it as a symbol of commitment. If anything, it was a sign of his belief that she should be independent. Automatically her breath came easier and her stomach settled and, even though a feeling of emptiness hollowed out her belly, she told herself it was just relief.

She turned to face him finally. 'Where are we going?'

'You'll see,' was all Pascal said. He was intent, quiet.

He'd told Alana to dress down and warmly. He'd brought a bag that looked like a gym bag, and must have thrown it in the boot as she couldn't see it anywhere now. She looked out the window and could see the picture-perfect Paris start to retreat, and as they veered onto a motorway with high graffiti-covered walls on either side, they left it behind completely.

After driving for about twenty minutes, Pascal took a slip road off the motorway, and the Paris he drove into now was a million miles from the Paris they'd just left. This was the suburbs. Unconsciously, Alana straightened in her seat and looked out at the bare streets, dilapidated buildings and bleak-looking, towering apartment-blocks in the distance.

'Is this where you grew up?'

He didn't look at her. He was grim. 'Near enough to here, yes.'

Groups of youths stood on the streets, along with women and children, going about their daily business. They passed a school and Alana could see children playing behind a high barbed-wire fence.

Pascal finally pulled into the car park of what looked like a well-kept community hall, but Alana guessed that it looked well kept thanks to the beefy security-guard posted on the gate who'd waved them through. Pascal parked and they got out. He still hadn't said anything, but Alana knew that he was watching her reaction closely, and suddenly it was very important to her that she pass whatever unspoken test was going on.

He grabbed his bag from the boot of the car, and just then a group of gangly, well-built youths burst from the hall. They surrounded them and the car in seconds, greeting Pascal with slang catcalls and jeers that must have been good-natured, as Pascal was smiling at them and answering back. He had her hand in a tight grip. A couple of the more menacing guys stood back and looked Alana up and down, and then walked round her, making comments. But she wasn't scared. If anything, she'd never felt safer with Pascal beside her, and even when one of the youths brushed close to her as if to test her reaction, and Pascal made a protective move, she gripped his hand to tell him it was OK. She knew this was a deeply ritualistic place, any kind of ghetto area was.

So she stood tall, even though they all towered over her, and after a long moment the tension was dissipated when the guys started laughing and one even clapped a hand on her shoulder. Pascal led her into the centre and sent her an enigmatic look before saying, *sotto voce*, 'You've just been accepted by one of the most notorious gang leaders in the area.'

She shivered then despite herself, because she knew well that being in one of these gangs meant life and death. Literally. Suddenly she could see how Pascal's move to live with his grandfather had undoubtedly changed the course of his life.

He left her alone for a few minutes under the watchful gaze of a kindly woman, who appeared to be the cook, and returned in faded sweats and a well-worn T-shirt. He was joined now by another huge well-built man who she recognised as a recently retired French international rugby-player. He'd featured in the last Six Nations tournament. He recognised Alana, too, and they spent a few minutes chatting amiably.

It was only when she followed them outside that she understood the full import of where they were and what was going on. It was a rugby pitch, and all of the youths she'd just met and many more were warming up and throwing rugby balls back and forth. Some were doing scrum-practice. Apart from Pascal and Mathieu, the retired player, there were also at least three coaches on hand. Pascal was in the thick of it, too, and all of Alana's suspicions were suspicions no longer. He had the easy athleticism of a top player.

The cook brought Alana a steaming cup of hot chocolate, and she settled down on a bench outside to watch, fascinated by how much raw talent was on the pitch in front of her.

A while later Pascal finally tore himself away from the action and sat down beside her, breathing heavily. His sweat-soaked and mucky clothes should have repelled her, but she found that all she could think about were his muscles—which she could imagine were hot and taut and gleaming after exertion—and the way his top clung to his stomach, clearly delineating his defined abdomen. She swallowed painfully and had to block a wanton desire to pull him into the hall behind them and beg him to make love to her. In all her years of avid sport watching, she'd never found a sweaty, mucky man arousing. Pregnancy hormones; that had to be it. She spoke as much to try and defuse her hectic pulse as anything else.

'I'm guessing this isn't just a few guys who come out here once a week to knock a ball around?'

He shook his head. 'They're part of a rugby academy I set up. I know at first glance they don't look it. I've set up a scholarship for kids who want to get to school or college through sport.' He shrugged. 'Rugby was always my love, so I've done it through that. I wanted to introduce the sport into the area.'

He looked at her then and she felt hot again.

'You were right—it is largely a middle-class game—but through something like this we're not letting it become exclusive. After all, I came from here, too.'

Her suspicions were confirmed. 'So you did want to play it too. Anyone watching you out there could see what a natural talent you have. Why didn't you go for it?'

He looked out to the men on the pitch and then spoke with a kind of resigned modesty. 'My grandfather could see how good I was. He had played all his life, and he was a great player. But it never got him anywhere. Originally he played it for acceptance into the community. He was half-Algerian, and he always felt like an outsider. That's why he took it so badly when my mother disgraced the good name he'd built up by having an affair with a married man.'

Alana looked at his profile. It was proud and harsh. A warrior's profile.

'He'd always regretted his actions towards her, so when she told him she was dying, he saw his chance to make it up to her and took me in. A few years after I'd started living with him and playing rugby, I was approached by a rugby scout, but my grandfather wouldn't let me go back to Paris to pursue the opportunity.'

'Why not?'

Pascal sighed. 'Because for one thing he didn't want me to end up in the suburbs again. He knew that if I got caught up in that world I might make it, I might be a star for a short time. But he also knew that ultimately I'd burn out and have nothing. It was only when I went to school in his village that I discovered I had a good brain. He saw it, too, and asked me to follow that route...college and a proper career. And not rugby.'

'You sacrificed your chance of a successful sports career to abide by your grandfather's wishes?'

He heard the incredulity in her voice and looked at her again, smiling ruefully, making something in her chest flip over. He jerked his head towards the pitch. 'These boys have brains too. I'm hoping that they get the best of both worlds. All my grandfather could see was one or the other. He was the only family member who showed a real interest in me. I couldn't turn my back on him.'

Alana shook her head, shocked at the level of sacrifice he'd made. It was so far removed from the kind of person her husband had been that her mind boggled.

His face sobered then, and he said quietly, 'The truth is that if I hadn't been taken in by my grandfather, there's a good chance I would have ended up in jail.' Alana held in a gasp and frowned slightly. His eyes were dark pools. She could sense that he was holding his emotions tightly in check.

'The gang I was with were getting more and more heavily involved with drugs, crime...we were the worst of the worst, Alana.' He gestured abruptly towards the field. 'The stuff we got up to makes these guys look like a girls' tea-party. I was on the periphery for a long time, but was about to be sucked right into the middle of it all. Part of the initiation rituals involved making a clear statement of intent, a show of bravery.'

'What do you mean?' Although Alana suspected she had a very good idea.

He looked away from her. 'The week after I left, a member of a rival gang was shot dead. If I'd still been there, I would've been picked to do the job; it was my turn.'

Alana grabbed his hand, making him face her. 'But you didn't do it, Pascal. You got out of here.' She had no idea how close he'd come to being lost for ever. She felt icy inside. She tried to show him that the horror she felt wasn't for what he'd been.

His face was bleak. He held up a hand, thumb and forefinger inches apart. 'Yes—but I was *this* close to doing it. That's scarier to acknowledge than you can imagine.'

Alana was fervent; she took his hand again. 'You can't say that for sure. You don't know what you would have done in that moment, what choice you would have made. Don't condemn yourself so easily.'

Pascal looked at her. Somewhere deep inside, he'd always felt as though another part of him still existed in this wasteland, lost for ever. Wild. Capable of awful things. But was she right? Would he have made another choice if he'd been faced with that scenario? Had he been carrying around the guilt all his life for something he wouldn't have even done?

He pulled his hand from hers, just as a rugby ball shot through the air towards them. Pascal stood easily and caught it deftly. He looked down at her for a long moment before turning and jogging back onto the pitch with easy grace. Alana felt a little shell shocked. She could only imagine how hard it must have been over the years to come to terms with how close to the edge he'd sailed. Or how painful it must have been to turn his back on something so dear to his heart for the sake of a family connection that had come so late in his life. She could see now that he'd channelled all of his ruthless, competitive energy into his professional life. It was no wonder he'd achieved what he had. And yet he hadn't become so embittered that he didn't want to help others achieve what he never had.

Later that afternoon they were in the car on the way home, dusk falling over the suburbs as they left them behind. 'So what did you think?' he asked innocuously.

Alana thought for a long moment before turning towards him. He'd showered with the guys in the community centre and changed, so thankfully her hormones had settled to their normal level of craziness around him. There was something deep inside her that begged to come out, some emotion, but it was too big for her to deal with. What he'd told her earlier was huge in its implications of a deepening intimacy between them, but she knew she was too cowardly to look at how it made her feel. She kept her voice light and deliberately stuck to neutral waters. 'I think what you're doing is amazing. Especially considering your own history. How many of those kids know how close you got to being a player?'

He shook his head. 'None. But Mathieu knows; we've been friends for years. He's from the same town as my grandfather. He was picked by the scout too. So, in a way, I got to follow his progress and see where he went.'

He looked at Alana before turning them back onto the motorway and seamlessly entering the manic Paris-bound traffic. 'My grandfather was right you know. Mathieu has this now—coaching, and perhaps some commentating—but apart from that he doesn't have much else. He's told me himself that sometimes he wishes he'd taken my path.'

Alana smiled. 'And you wish you could have taken his.'

Pascal shrugged. 'Who knows if I really missed out on all that much?'

After a companionable silence Alana could feel tiredness wash over her, and she stifled a yawn. She couldn't help sinking down a little into the comfort of the seat. She felt safe and protected and warm. And before she knew it, she was slipping into a welcoming dark abyss. So she didn't see when Pascal looked over, and she didn't see the intense look on his face as his eyes swept down over her body. And she only had the barest of sensations when he reached over and tucked some wayward hair behind her ear.

Pascal tore his eyes away from Alana as she fell easily into sleep. He couldn't believe he'd revealed so much earlier, even though he'd intended to tell her about his life, his past. But it had been easy. And she hadn't looked at him with horror, she'd understood. He couldn't even begin to fathom how that could be possible when she'd lived such a different life—a secure life, loved and surrounded by a big family. Telling her had been like letting go of a huge weight around his shoulders.

He glanced at her again, his chest tight with emotion. She was his now. He knew that he never wanted to let her go, that he would do whatever it took to show her that they had something beyond the physical. That they had something that could work, that could last. And to do that all he had to do was avoid the physical. He grimaced. When every part of him burned up just looking at her, he knew it would be the hardest thing he'd ever done—yet at that moment it was the only way he knew how to show her, to demonstrate to her his intention.

Alana woke the following morning to find herself naked but for her underwear in her bed, and she couldn't believe it when the clock said 10:00 a.m. She'd slept for the entire previous evening and night. Had Pascal undressed her? Who else could it have been? And she'd slept through it?

She showered and dressed quickly, feeling completely dis-orientated. When she emerged into the main drawing room after finding no note in the kitchen, she jumped with fright when Pascal's study-door opened and he strode out, dressed head to toe in his successful-billionaire gear. A world away from the mucky rugby coach of yesterday. Her heart clenched.

She folded her arms defensively, not sure why she was feeling like that. Prickly. 'I'm sorry, I was obviously more exhausted than I thought. It must be the pregnancy.'

Pascal stopped a few feet away from her; he looked so stern and grim that Alana felt a little scared.

'It's me who should be sorry,' he surprised her by saying. 'I shouldn't have had you sitting out on a cold bench all day. You could have caught cold or anything. How are you feeling? I think we should go to see the doctor just in case. I was going to call her if you didn't wake up soon.'

Alana couldn't help laughing, and it completely defused the tension she was feeling. 'Pascal! Don't be ridiculous; I'm fine. I'm a hardy Irish girl. Sitting on a cold bench for a few hours will not bring on early labour or pneumonia.'

'All the same…' He looked genuinely worried, and Alana's heart clenched again. She rolled her eyes, ignoring her worrying reaction; maybe something *was* wrong with her? 'Pascal, really, I haven't slept that well the last few nights, I'm sure that's all it was. Here—' she reached out, took his hand and brought it to her forehead '—see? No fever. I'm fine.'

His hand felt warm and strong on her head, and she could feel his pulse at his wrist. It had an immediate effect on her body, and she felt herself respond, her own pulse tripping. She hurriedly took his hand down again. If she kept it there, she *would* feel feverish in a minute. She stepped back to put some space between them and he looked utterly unmoved by the physical contact. She was still confused by this wall, this distance, that existed between them. It had to be because he just didn't find her attractive any more, and that was becoming harder for her to bear than she'd imagined it would be.

He finally seemed to be satisfied that she was OK, and

started to walk back to his study, throwing over his shoulder, 'I've lined up some places for us to look at today.'

Alana followed him, glad of the distraction from her roiling emotions and hormones. 'Places? What do you mean?'

She followed him into his light, airy study and looked around with interest. Shelves from floor to ceiling were packed with all sorts of books. A huge table stood in one corner, where he told her he sometimes held impromptu meetings. It was a hub of energy, but Alana knew that once Pascal walked out, the energy would dissipate.

He was round the other side of his desk, and he gestured for her to come and have a look at something on the computer screen. She walked over feeling a little apprehensive and tried to stay as far away from his body heat as possible.

'What am I meant to be looking at?'

He pressed a key, and what looked like a property page came up with pictures of houses and gardens.

'These are all houses and apartments for sale around Paris, mostly around Montmartre. You mentioned that you liked that area.'

'I…well…I know, but what do you mean? Why are we looking at these?' He looked at her as if she were slightly dim, and she could feel herself getting hot.

'I don't think that this place is going to be ideal for when the baby comes, do you? Even though we have the lift, we're on the top floor, and it's hardly kitted out to accommodate a baby.'

Alana started to back away, her belly churning again. No, she could imagine very well that this wouldn't suit him. This apartment screamed 'billionaire bachelor'. There was no room for a baby. Alana still felt a little too stunned to say anything else but, 'I guess you're right.'

'Good. Now, I've arranged some viewings for today, if that's OK?' He didn't wait for an answer, he strode over, took her arm and herded her out of his study. 'You should have some breakfast and then we'll head out to see them.'

By that evening Alana's head was spinning. She'd seen stunning art-deco ground-floor apartments in the Latin Quarter. She'd seen beautiful town houses in Montmartre, with idyllic gardens tucked away from prying eyes. She'd seen opulent, airy, studio-style apartments near the Eiffel Tower. Then she'd seen some more in the upmarket eighteenth-*arrondissement*. All of them had the same thing in common: they were all exclusive and awe-inspiringly, jaw-droppingly expensive. The *crème de la crème* of Paris real-estate. When she'd hissed to Pascal about the cost, he'd waved her concerns away and talked over her head to the agents about what it would take to make the properties baby-safe.

Clearly setting up his ex-lover and his baby in a suitable pad was something he was prepared to pay for. And it was also quite clear to Alana that Pascal meant to live in his own apartment and have her living independently, complete with family car, just across town or around the corner; if she liked the first apartment they'd looked at that morning. But she didn't think he'd be too thrilled at the prospect of running into her and the baby with his new lover. There had been no talk of 'we'; it had been all down to her to say if she liked a place or not.

Her life had transformed so completely in such a short space of time that Alana felt light headed as they walked back into Pascal's apartment. Compounding everything had been his careful restraint from touching her all day. Even if she'd brushed off him, he'd moved away as if he couldn't bear to be near her. She stopped dead inside the door and Pascal glanced back at her briefly. 'I have a business dinner to attend tonight. I'd ask you along, if you want, but I'm sure you're tired after today.'

Alana could have laughed. She had so much adrenaline

running through her body at that moment that she felt she could run a marathon.

'I'm fine.' She pushed herself off the door. 'Tell me, have you done this before? You seem to have everything pretty well arranged for setting us up.'

He turned fully then and looked at her suspiciously. 'Us?'

Alana's hand went to her belly. A fear of the isolation that lay in store for her made her feel panicky. 'Me and the baby. How do you know I even want to live here permanently, Pascal? I never said I wanted to live here. I told you, I fully expect to go home at some stage.'

He turned away in an abrupt negation of her words. 'Don't be ridiculous. You're having my baby; I told you, I'm going to be involved every step of the way.'

The fear rose up even stronger. 'Just as long as we're on opposite sides of the city, you mean.'

He turned again, his mouth a thin line of displeasure. 'What are you talking about, Alana? I don't have time for this.'

'Well, neither do I.' Alana could feel tears sting her eyes. All she did want right then, despite the evidence of his lack of desire, was for Pascal to stop this autocratic confusing behaviour, walk over and pull her into his arms, to tip her face up to his and kiss her deeply and soundly until she didn't have to think any more—and certainly until she didn't have to think about becoming a rich man's brood mare, relegated to the sidelines. However lonely things had got with Ryan, at least there had been the pretence of some kind of union, togetherness. And yet she knew she didn't want that, either. Her head was so fried that it hurt. And it was all this man's fault. She glared at him.

Pascal stepped towards her as if to say something, and his mobile rang abruptly. With a muttered curse, he pulled it out of his pocket and turned away to speak rapidly. Alana walked past him and into the kitchen. After a few minutes he came to the door. He looked and sounded weary, and Alana's heart lurched before she clamped down on the rogue impulse to worry about him or tell him he looked tired. She'd been a wife before; she would not do that again. And especially not with a man like Pascal.

'Look, I have to go out now, they've moved dinner forward. We'll talk tomorrow, OK?'

Alana sent him an airy, 'Fine,' and she resolutely turned away and started opening doors and drawers at random. When she stopped and looked around again, he had gone.

## CHAPTER NINE

AS SOON as she knew she was alone, the tears came, and through them Alana ranted at herself—what was wrong with her? She wanted Pascal and yet she didn't want him. She wanted to be independent, and then when he brought her out to show her places where she could live independently, she didn't want that, either.

All she knew for sure, as she wiped away the tears and prepared some dinner, was that she *wanted* him with a bone-deep ache that ran through her body like a dull pain. It got worse every time he came near. She'd been having erotic dreams nearly every night about what had happened in the restaurant, waking with sheets damp and twisted around her body. She needed the physical. It was as if that would make all her confusion go away, if she could just bury herself in that release that only he could give her...

As Alana sat and ate, not tasting any of it, an intense desire rose up within her to seduce Pascal, making it hard to think of anything else. Her blood felt heavy and her pulse throbbed. She told herself she had to know for sure if he was simply not attracted to her any more. If that was the case it would make things so much easier. She would go home and face the music. She wouldn't let him set her up in Paris like some ex-mistress. But she had to know. Feeling much better all of a sudden, Alana hopped down from the stool, washed up her plates and headed for her shower.

She hummed and hawed over what to wear, and then she found herself going into Pascal's room. She opened up his wardrobe and his scent reached out and enveloped her. Her pulse sped up to triple time and her breathing quickened; he didn't even have to be here in person and he could turn her on. She shook her head and reached in to pull out one of his silk ties. She'd seen a scene in a movie once that involved a woman waiting for her man dressed in nothing but a tie, but Alana didn't think she had the balls for that, especially with the slight thickening of her waistline. So she pulled out a shirt too.

Dressed in the shirt and tie, she left her hair down and put on the slightest amount of make-up, just enough to enhance her eyes. Feeling slightly silly but quashing it, she pulled on pants at the last minute, and then she got a bottle of wine with a glass and went into the sitting room to wait.

The minutes ticked by, and Alana alternately felt confident, bolshy, insecure and then gravitated back to feeling silly again. But she was determined to stick it out. She needed him too badly. She needed to know too badly. Even if he rejected her, it would be better than this awful ambiguity, this wall of distance. She had to put a stop to the way things seemed to be escalating out of her control, as if Pascal knew something she didn't, as if he was reading from a different script.

She made herself some hot chocolate. She opened the wine to let it breathe. She watched the news. She watched a French film and couldn't understand a word. The shirt started feeling constrictive, so she opened the top button and loosened the tie. And in the end she could feel tiredness washing over her. She fought it for a long time, but the cushions were so luxurious it was hard not to sink into them a little, to just close her eyes for a few minutes. Confident that she would hear him coming in, she let herself doze.

When Pascal let himself quietly into the apartment he became alert immediately. The light was on in the sitting room, so he went in there. He stopped in his tracks and the breath locked in his chest at the sight in front of him. Alana was asleep on the couch. Dressed in one of his shirts and ties. Long, bare legs flung out, hair in disarray around her head, one hand on her belly, the other by her head, palm up. All at once innocent and so wickedly sensuous that he felt dizzy with lust.

He barely took in the full bottle of wine and the glass, the empty mug of something. He came close, but didn't want to break the spell. Had she dressed like this on purpose for him? He shrugged off his jacket and undid his tie, barely aware of what he was doing. He felt constricted, and his body was so hard and so hot that time seemed to stand still. She was temptation incarnate. Her lips were soft, inviting him to just bend down and press a kiss. It would be so easy to do that—to kneel here beside her, to slip his tongue between those lips, have her wake and take his tongue deeper into her mouth, mimicking the way she would take another part of him deep inside her.

Pascal fought the most intense battle as he stood there. The memory of undressing her as clinically as he could the other night was still fresh and painful in his memory. But his resolve was strong. He could exert it again even if he felt like it would kill him. With his face set in rigid lines of ultimate control, a control he hadn't had to call on before, he bent down and slipped his arms underneath her pliant, sleep-relaxed body. She made a small sound, a mere breath, and her body automatically curved into him as he lifted her up effortlessly. Her breasts pressed against his chest. Pascal had to stop for a moment and grit his jaw so hard that it hurt. He was so aroused that he didn't think he'd make it to her bedroom. But he had to. He was doing this for *them*.

Alana knew she was fighting her way through layers of sleep for a reason. She felt so safe and so secure that she wanted to stay there for ever. And yet, another feeling was making her wake up, something within her, an urgency that was starting down low in her abdomen and spreading outwards, making everything tingle deliciously. She finally started to wake as she became aware of being carried in strong arms against a hard, muscled chest. *Pascal.* And at that moment he was putting her down, letting her go. Every part of her screamed rejection at that.

'Wait, what are you doing?' she asked, still feeling drowsy.

His voice rumbled low and near her ear, setting off another chain reaction of sensations, waking her more. 'You're half-asleep. You should go back to sleep, Alana.'

'But…' Alana struggled through the waves that wanted to suck her back down. 'I stayed up to seduce you.' She knew somewhere rational that it was only because it was dark and she was still half-asleep that she was being so honest.

Pascal's body tensed, she could feel it as he rested momentarily over her on his hands after depositing her on her bed. Finally, after a long moment, he just said enigmatically, 'You only have to look at me and I'm seduced. Go to sleep, Alana.'

He stood and swiftly left the room, and suddenly Alana was wide-awake and alert. She sat up in the bed, in the dark. *You only have to look at me and I'm seduced.* Had she dreamt that? She didn't think so, she'd felt the tension in his body; it was the same tension running through her right now.

She threw back the covers and got out of the bed. With her heart thumping, she went back out to the sitting room, where she instinctively knew he'd be. She stopped at the door. He was standing at the window, one hand deep in the pocket of his trousers, pulling the material taut over one buttock, and she could see the wineglass was gone. Just then his head tipped back and she saw him drink deeply from the claret liquid.

She saw the lines of tension come into his body before he turned round, and a part of her hated that tension. Alana crossed her arms. His eyes were narrowed, his face had that stern expression, but she couldn't let that stop her.

'What's that supposed to mean—you only have to look at me to be seduced? So if that's the case, then why…?' She couldn't say it, even now, even after waiting up to seduce him.

'Why don't I make love to you?' he asked harshly.

Alana nodded jerkily. He put down his glass and now both hands were deep in his pockets, his frame huge and powerful, awe-inducing. Alana felt that ever-present quiver in her belly.

'Because I was attempting to show you that what we can have is more than just…lust, desire, *sex*.'

Alana shook her head and walked a little closer. 'I don't understand.'

Pascal took out a hand and raked it through his hair, mussing it up, making him look even more rakishly attractive.

'From the moment we've met it's been about physical attraction, unprecedented physical attraction, for the both of us.'

She flushed.

'But now that you're pregnant, we're having a baby and I just wanted to try and elevate things to another level. The way you make me feel… That evening in the restaurant, I had no intention of allowing things to get that far, but within seconds we couldn't turn back.' That lack of control still stung him.

Alana's flush deepened. She saw Pascal's eyes narrow even more on her face, and a stain of colour washed his cheeks too. The air around them was saturated with their desire. Alana didn't know how she was still standing. She felt weak and trembly. And a little angry.

'What are you talking about, Pascal—elevating things to another level? We're just... We were lovers. I'm here while things settle down at home. Nothing's changed.'

He crossed his arms at that, and his face got even sterner. 'Why do you keep saying that? I've told you, we're together now. I'm not going to be apart from you or this baby.'

Bitterness and something else indefinable washed up through Alana. 'And yet you've spent the day showing me places where you'll happily shelve me and our child.' She shook her head. 'I won't have that, Pascal. I'd prefer to go home than become just your responsibility.'

He came towards her, stopping her words, a look of exasperation crossing his face. 'What are you talking about? The places we looked at today are for the three of us, not just you and the baby. What made you think that?'

At that moment he could have knocked Alana down with a feather. She just looked at him. He read her in an instant.

'Did you really think I was going to go on living here and have you living a separate life in another part of the city?' His eyes glittered and he was so close now that Alana could touch him if she wanted. But right now, for the first time, she didn't want to. She backed away.

'Yes, I did think that. We've never discussed this, Pascal. I told you I was happy with no commitment. But just...not like this...' That panicky feeling was surging back, a painful vicelike feeling around her heart. He made her feel so confused, so mixed up.

'That was before you got pregnant. Things are different now.'

'But I don't want that. My God,' she breathed as she finally saw what he had been doing. The suspicion she'd had when she'd seen the car, the way it had made her feel, surged back to haunt her now. 'The car, the apartments... You've been planning this all along, haven't you?'

'Well, one of us has to face the reality, Alana. Tell me, how *do* you see the future for you, me and our baby?'

'I see me going home as soon as I can, and you can visit whenever you want.' Her voice sounded high and constricted to her ears. At that moment she also knew that any feelings about her precious independence being threatened were so flimsy it was laughable. To acknowledge that fact now made her feel even more exposed. If her independence, which she'd guarded so zealously after Ryan's death, could so easily be forgotten, then what did that mean?

He advanced and she backed away. This was exactly what she didn't want to look at; she didn't want to have to clarify her feelings. She knew now that was why she'd craved the physical contact so badly. She'd sensed he had an agenda. He'd been intent on weaving her into the fabric of his life with an ease that scared her. He was threatening the very foundation of her life, the life she'd built so carefully after Ryan died. She shook her head, begging him silently to understand.

'Can you honestly tell me that when I'm like a beached whale, you'll still be happy with me in your life? That when we have a screaming baby waking every hour on the hour for feeds, that you'll not regret failing to maintain your independence?' His relentless advancing goaded her further, making her lash out. 'Or perhaps you're planning on keeping this apartment and having it for your mistresses? Well, I won't stand for that, either.'

He finally caught up with her and grabbed her arms in his hands; they burned through the thin material, and it was only then that Alana became aware of how she was still dressed in his shirt and tie. It mocked her now, the thought that she could have used the physical to avoid talking about this.

'Dammit, Alana, I won't live up to the box you want to put me in. I have no intention of taking a mistress. I was going to sell this place.' He laughed harshly, and the sound grated on Alana's nerves. 'I never thought I'd say this, but for the first time in my life, I've even contemplating marriage— you've made me believe that perhaps it can be different for me, *us*, despite our pasts. Although I know the mere mention of it would send you running. So I've been bending over backwards to try and show you that we can have a life here, that we can have something that's not just about sex. I'm prepared to commit to you, but you won't even give the thought of family life a chance, not even for our child.'

Alana was starting to shake. His words... What was he saying? It was too much for her to deal with. 'But you...you're a playboy. You like being single. You don't do this. How can you want this?' A treacherous flutter of hope mocked her loudly amidst the panic.

'When you're the *woman* and you don't?' he asked caustically. He laughed then, harshly, his hands still around her arms. Every small hair seemed to stand on edge along Alana's skin. She saw his eyes drop to take in her attire, and her breasts felt heavy and sensitive. She'd thought he'd killed her desire with all his words and scary rationale, but now it was flaming back, yet she wanted to fight it. But Pascal, it seemed, had other ideas.

His mouth was a cruel line. 'It seems an awful pity to waste this, after all.' He ran a long finger around her jaw and down to the pulse beating hectically in her throat.

'No, Pascal, not like this; you don't want this.'

'Don't I?' He arched a cynical brow. 'You seem to know me so well, Alana. You think that I'd be turned off by your pregnant, blooming body, or that I'd hate to hear my own baby call for food, that I'd hate to take it in turns to do night feeds to give you a break. That I'd grow tired of domestic life, that I'd keep this place to house my mistresses. As you seem to know me so well, perhaps you'll also know that I'm done with talking. I'm done with trying to show you another side to this relationship when clearly all you're interested in is physical gratification. It never went beyond that for you, did it?'

Before Alana could take in his words, before she could formulate anything, even a thought, as the hurt rippled through her, he brought his hands to the tie and pulled it open and off in a fluid move. Then he brought his hands to her shirt, *his* shirt, and calmly, without violence, ripped it open. Alana gasped as the air whistled over her naked breasts and buttons popped and fell to the floor, scattering loudly.

'Right now, I'm also done with denying myself what you're so generously offering.'

With that Pascal hauled Alana's semi-naked body into his, one hand around her back, the other spearing through her hair as his mouth drove down onto hers, taking and plundering. Her world became a ball of fire that she couldn't step away from, even though she knew it was going to burn her badly. After so much build up Alana was helpless not to respond, even though she knew in some small, still-rational part of her brain that it would be much better for her to step back and say no. But her body had other ideas. Her hands were already scrabbling for his shirt, pulling it out of his trousers. She was aching to feel his skin. She reached for buttons, found them and opened them impatiently, and somehow managed to push the shirt off his broad shoulders where it fell to the floor unseen and already forgotten beside hers.

Pascal pulled back, breathing harshly. 'You turn me into something... You make me feel like I've still got my past in my blood. Like I'm untamed.'

Alana reached up a hand and curved it around his jaw. Everything that had just happened previously was forgotten. 'It's not a bad thing, it's a part of you.' She reached up and pressed a kiss to his jaw, and she felt it clench. 'I can handle it. Show me what it's like.'

Pascal bent and lifted Alana into his arms, striding into her bedroom and depositing her on the bed. He ripped off the rest of his clothes and then he was standing in front of her, naked and massively aroused. Alana sat up on the side of the bed and reached for him, pulling him to her. She looked up at him as her hand closed around his hard length and as she took him into her mouth.

She could feel that he was trying to control himself. He brought a hand to her head; she felt it shaking. But he wouldn't let her bring him to the edge or beyond. He stopped her and pulled back, and then his big hands reached underneath and lifted her bodily back onto the bed. With a flick of his wrist, he smoothed her pants down and off her legs. He ran a hand over the slight swell of her belly, the only indication of their child growing within. He pressed a kiss to it, and inexplicably Alana felt tears threaten. As if to drive the emotion away, she reached down and pulled Pascal up her body. She could see a harsh glitter in his eyes, as if he knew what she was doing.

'Please,' she begged, opening her legs around him, feeling his weight and strength between them. 'I want you now.'

He rested over her on his hands for a long moment and Alana bit her lip. She couldn't take her eyes away from his; she knew there was a silent battle of wills going on. But finally, just when she thought he was going to make her beg, he slipped a hand under her buttocks, tilting her up towards him, and then with one deep, cataclysmic thrust, he entered her and she felt as if he'd touched her soul.

She wrapped her legs around him as far as she could, drawing him in deeper and deeper, going with him when he pulled out, and drawing him in tight again when he thrust back. She reached up and wrapped her arms around his neck, her mouth blindly finding and pressing kisses to any bit of exposed flesh, and he took them higher and higher. When the pinnacle came after an excruciatingly exquisite climb, Alana reached a hand down to his buttock and with her other held on tight as the waves of pleasure and release washed through her. She felt his own release burst free inside her, as his back tautened and tensed. His whole body was rigid as helpless after-shocks rushed through him too.

He came down over her and rolled them so that he lay on his side. Their breath mingled, and came harsh and swift. Alana was tucked into his chest, his weight off her belly. Still entwined with Pascal from arms down to legs, intimately joined, Alana fell immediately into a deep sleep, not even waking when Pascal extricated himself, or moved her under the covers or left her alone in the bed to go back to his own room. He sent one brief glance back to her in the bed, the set of his features grim.

The next morning when Alana woke, she had a delicious feeling of satisfaction. She was aware of pleasureable aches and pains throughout her body before the entire previous night came back in vivid recall. Instantly, the warm feeling seeped away and she tensed. Even though she was lying down, the world spun on its axis for a moment.

She didn't have to look to know that Pascal hadn't spent the night in the bed with her. She didn't hear any sounds from the apartment. Getting up, she grimaced when she felt tender. After washing and dressing, she went outside, but she knew Pascal had gone to work. She found a note in the kitchen:

We need to talk.
Pascal.

Fear and trepidation rushed through Alana's body as she recalled everything that had preceded their explosive love-making the previous night. Had he really told her that he

wanted to make a go of this, create a proper family life? He'd
even said that he'd respect her wish not to marry, knowing
that she wouldn't want that. But that truth rocked her: he'd
contemplated *marriage*?

Pascal was offering her security, more than just an exten-
sion of their affair. She knew she couldn't keep ignoring the
fact that strings were very much a part of it now. Her hand
went to her belly; they weren't strings, they were ropes,
binding her and Pascal together for ever whether she liked it
or not.

That panicky feeling was back, and even stronger this
time. It threatened to consume Alana utterly. Feeling claustrophobic, she picked up the apartment keys and went out to
walk. Anything to try and clear her head.

She came back later, feeling just as muddled as ever. When
her mobile phone rang, she picked it up gratefully, wanting
any distraction, even if it was her sister Ailish, to take her
away from her tortured conscience. But it wasn't her sister.
After talking to the person on the other end for a few minutes,
she terminated the call. It was a sign—a welcome sign. Pascal
didn't know what he was talking about, offering her this life.
She'd seen it before. He'd change to adapt, but ultimately he
would revert back to what he was.

And Alana didn't want to look at why that cut her so
deeply. She told herself it was because she couldn't put herself
through trusting someone again, but in her heart of hearts she
knew she wasn't being honest with herself. That was only the
half of it.

'I'm flying home tonight, Pascal, on the late flight from
Charles de Gaulle. It's all booked. I've got a taxi coming any
minute.'

Pascal stood just inside the door of the living room where
Alana had been waiting to confront him all afternoon. And

now she'd blurted the words out with little or no finesse. They hung baldly in the air between them.

Pascal looked utterly cold and remote. This was what Alana had had a glimpse of when she'd first met him, the side of him she'd always thought would be formidable. And it was. He put down his attaché case and walked over to the drinks cabinet on the opposite side of the room. He poured himself a neat drink of something powerful before turning back to Alana.

'What do you want me to say, Alana?'

She crossed her arms even tighter across her chest as if she could stop her heart beating and feeling so much pain. Pain that she still denied to herself. 'I don't want you to say anything. You don't have to say anything.'

He gave a short, curt laugh and downed the liquid in one, before turning back to pour himself another. 'No, I forgot. You're not into conversation, are you? I tried that. I think all you want is a gigolo.'

'Stop that. That's unfair.'

'Oh, really? And how is it that our best communication was in bed last night?'

Alana blanched.

'Look, I appreciate what you wanted to do.'

His voice was icy. 'Don't patronise me, Alana. Do what you want, but don't do that. I'm not asking you to marry me.' He ran a hand through his hair, the first signs of anger coming out. 'God forbid I might do that! I'm offering you everything on a plate. And a chance to build a life together for the sake of a family. Not even your husband offered you that.'

'Don't bring him into this.'

'Why not?' Pascal taunted. 'Isn't he the reason you've got that Fort Knox of defences around you? The reason you won't let anyone close, not even the father of your unborn child?'

'There's more to it than that,' Alana gritted out, shamingly aware that Pascal spoke the truth. She felt cornered again, panicky. 'What you've been doing is tantamount to…a…a deception. You could have told me what you had in mind, but you let me believe that you wanted to set me up as some sort of mistress. And then you bring me out to the suburbs and make me see what you're doing, tell me about your past…' Alana couldn't stop the incoherent jumble of thoughts spilling out. 'It's almost as if you're trying to get me to—' *Fall in love with you…* The words flashed into her head and she stopped, stunned. She knew they were wrong, but that word *'love'* made her feel weak. Even more claustrophobic.

Pascal stayed where he was, rocking back on his heels, surveying her coolly. 'To what, Alana? *Trust* me? Is that it?' He downed the rest of the liquid and slammed the glass down, making her flinch. 'Is that such a crime?'

Alana shook her head; her arms felt numb now, she held them across her body so tight. 'No…it's not. I'm sorry, I just can't…can't do this. With you.'

'You can't trust me, you mean. You can't even try. And what do you think is waiting for you back in Dublin? No job, a family you don't confide in and a mortgage you're hardly equipped to start paying off again.'

Alana winced at his condemnation. She hitched up her chin. 'I had a call from Rory earlier. He's offered me my job back. Eoin Donohoe's wife came out and revealed the truth behind their marriage. She's seeking a divorce now too. And some of the women who were with Ryan have come out and sold their stories. So, you see, I can go back now.' It sounded weak and pathetic to her ears, but she'd never been so grateful for an escape route.

Pascal's mouth twisted. 'How fortunate. And what do you think you're going to do about our child?'

Alana felt bleak and hollow inside. 'I told you from the

start, you can have as much access as you want. I'd never deny you that, Pascal.'

Just then the doorbell rang. It was obviously the concierge ringing up to tell her that the taxi was outside. Alana moved forward on wooden legs. She avoided Pascal's eye, but just when she drew alongside him, he gripped her arm and pulled her round.

'I *am* the father of your child, and I won't have you sideline me. I can't lock you in here. If you want to go, then go, but I'm not going to come running after you. I don't chase women.' His eyes burnt right through her with a fierce black intensity.

'I know,' she said through stiff lips. *This was it.* Already she could feel herself anticipating the pain of one day seeing him with someone new, but she had to bury it deep, because if she even thought of that for a second now, she wouldn't make it out the door.

# CHAPTER TEN

'HEY, Alana, nice to have you back, we missed you.'

Alana smiled at Sophie, but it felt forced as she walked into her old office. 'Thanks.'

She closed the door behind her. Everything had felt wan since she'd come home just a few days ago. She felt listless, as if a vital source of energy had been taken from her body. She smiled bleakly to herself. She knew what that was: *Pascal*. She sat down behind her desk heavily.

Just then a knock came on her door, and before she could answer, it opened and Rory barrelled in. 'Alana! Great to have you back. Sorry about all that business before, but you know my hands were tied.'

Alana couldn't help a wry smile as Rory's words flowed into one another and washed over her aching head.

'…Pascal Lévêque for the charity bash in the K Club this weekend.'

Alana's body straightened up as if she'd been given a shot of adrenaline. 'What did you say?' Her heart was already beating fast. Out of control.

Rory rolled his eyes. 'I was talking about the Rugby fund-raising party at the weekend. It's at the K Club in Kildare. Your friend Lévêque is hosting it.' The K Club was an exclusive golf club and hotel about an hour out of Dublin. The rich and famous regularly helicoptered in for a few days there. Alana felt her blood run cold. 'Rory, you don't want me to cover it, do you?'

She could have wept with relief when he said, 'No, I think it's still a bit soon to put you at the forefront of such a high-profile event.' He laughed nervously. 'Never know who you might run into!'

He rambled on for a bit about what he wanted her to concentrate on, and Alana was relieved when he got up to go. He stopped at the door though, and looked back for a minute, his eyes shrewd on hers. 'I suppose things didn't work out with Lévêque?'

Alana felt protectively for her belly, which seemed to be swelling each day now. She shook her head quickly and forced a smile.

Rory smiled too. 'I'm sure it's for the best. He's not exactly in our league, is he?'

Alana shook her head again and held her breath till Rory left. When he did she sagged like a rag doll.

Hearing Rory mention his name now had somehow finally made Alana face up to the reaction that still held her body in its grip. She'd known it all along, if she was honest with herself, she'd just been in a pathetic state of denial.

She loved him. She loved him so much that even to think about it or acknowledge it made her feel dizzy. It was all so clear now, and what came with the clarity wasn't panic, or claustrophobia; they had all been symptoms of the futile denial of her feelings. She actually felt relief, relief for being honest with herself for the first time in weeks.

She'd craved the physical contact with Pascal in order to feel connected to him without having to look at her feelings. When he'd maintained that ridiculous distance, it had nearly killed her. The extent to which he'd been prepared to commit to her still made her shake, and she knew that walking away hadn't been a fear of commitment or a lack of trust—it had been the fear that he didn't love her, that he'd been doing it solely out of a sense of responsibility. He'd turned his back on his dream of becoming a rugby sporting-hero to fulfil his grandfather's wishes. So Alana knew he was capable of making big sacrifices. But she didn't want to be a sacrifice.

That was what it came down to. Ultimately she had to concede now that Ryan had never truly killed her spirit. He'd only dampened it. Meeting Pascal had brought it back to life. But she wanted him to love her too. She could do anything if she had that, even contemplate getting married again; she knew that now. Her real fear had been of committing to a life with Pascal only to witness his inevitable decline in interest and his taking of a mistress or leaving her.

Yet, was she being unfair? He'd already accused her of trying to read his mind and she'd got it spectacularly wrong. Could she risk it? Could she put her heart on her sleeve and walk away in one piece if he said 'no thanks'?

Somehow, Alana knew that, whether or not she could survive his rejection, she owed it to herself and their baby at least to be honest. Properly honest. The only thing was, it could already be too late.

'Look, Alana, I'm sorry but I don't know where he is. He's probably gone to a club in town or something. He was here earlier and now he's not, OK?' Rory shrugged apologetically, too wound up and hyper even to ask her why she was looking for Pascal. He hurried off again.

Alana stood inside the main reception door of the K Club. She could see the glittering dresses of the women through the doors of the main ballroom in the distance, the men in their tuxedos. And somehow she knew Rory was right; he wasn't there. She left and got back into her car outside the main door. It had taken all of her guts just to drive down to the K Club, and now this. She'd asked at Reception, and after much cajoling Alana had found out that he was booked in there for the night.

A part of her knew she should wait for him to return, but another part of her urged herself to follow a hunch. She knew if she was wrong, then she was going miles in the opposite direction, but she turned her car round and headed back for Dublin anyway.

The security-guard at the gates of Croke Park recognised her and let her in, saying, 'What is it about this place tonight? It's not as if there's a match on.'

Alana felt hope bloom in her chest, and it solidified when she drove in and saw the familiar lines of a sleek black Lexus. With a palpitating heart and clammy hands, she got out of her car and walked in through the dark tunnel to get to the pitch.

*He was here.*

Alana's heart clenched painfully. He was sitting on a seat up near the press and VIP boxes, looking out broodily into the moonlit pitch. He looked darkly mysterious, his tuxedo visible underneath a black overcoat. At that point her heart swelled in her chest. She'd never felt that happen when she'd looked at Ryan. So much was different, and that was what she had to trust. She was stronger now, clear for the first time in her life. If he didn't love her the way she loved him, then she'd let him go. But she at least owed it to him to let him know why she wouldn't commit to him: she couldn't without his love.

She walked up the steps and then into his row of seats. He seemed lost in another world. Her foot scuffed a discarded plastic cup, and at that he looked up. Alana stopped in her tracks, just feet away. She was very aware of her old jeans, woollen jumper and jacket, hair down and blowing in the breeze. She couldn't read the expression on his face, but she could see the deep grooves beside his mouth. His eyes flicked dispassionately over her before he turned away again.

'What are you doing here?'

The harshness of his tone made her quail inside, but she wouldn't let it daunt her.

'I was looking for you.'

He gave a sort of curt laugh and stared fixedly back out to the pitch. 'Correct me if I'm wrong, but I think the last time we saw each other you couldn't wait to see the back of me.'

Alana forced herself to move forward and sat into the seat beside him. She could feel him move his body away imperceptibly. Her hands were clenched deep inside the pockets of her coat. One hand was curled around what she'd brought with her, and it burned like a mocking brand into the palm of her hand.

She fixed on a point out in the pitch and took a deep breath. 'I'd like to tell you something.'

She felt him shrug one powerful shoulder near her but then he stood up. Alana acted on instinct and whipped out a hand, catching his. She looked up at him.

'Please. Hear me out.'

With a hard expression, no emotion, he took his hand from hers. She held her breath and let it out again unsteadily when he finally sat again, clearly tense.

She forced herself to speak. 'I never really loved Ryan. I grew up believing in the sanctity of marriage. I grew up believing that that was what I wanted, to be like the rest of my family. When we met, Ryan swept me off my feet, made me believe in the dream. He told me he wouldn't stop me working, but then he did. He told me we'd be happy, but we weren't. And the thing was, by the time doubts were crowding my head just days before the wedding, I couldn't stop it. So much money had been spent, so much emotion invested. My parents were old. I knew they wanted to see me settled before it was too late. And I just…I couldn't stop it. I knew I was making a mistake. I'd isolated myself spectacularly in a bubble of make believe. And yet still I hoped for the best, put my trust in what I'd witnessed growing up, thought everything would work out OK.'

Alana felt Pascal turn towards her, but couldn't look at him. Her eyes stung with tears but her voice didn't waver. 'I was a baby, Pascal, just twenty-two. I hardly knew myself, never mind Ryan. I subjugated myself, put myself through hell with him to try and make things work, and I just...I just couldn't believe how easily I'd let someone like him take over my life. I should have seen it. I should have had more self-respect to know—'

Pascal reached out and took her hand that was twisting on her knee, stopping her words. Stopping her heart. She still couldn't look at him.

'Alana, look at me.'

Very reluctantly, she turned her head. His eyes were dark and molten, like she hadn't seen them for a long time, and she wanted to dive right in and drown in their depths, but she held herself rigid. She had so much more to say. He spoke before she could.

'You said it yourself, you were so young and you obviously felt you had to live up to the expectations of your own family.'

She nodded jerkily, relieved that he was stalling her for a moment. 'I know, I know that now. And I can't regret it, because it taught me so much. I know now, too, that my family would have been there for me if I'd confided in them. But I just always felt so distant, removed from them, like I couldn't go and bother them with my petty problems.'

Pascal shook his head. 'They weren't petty.'

'I know that now, too,' Alana said quietly.

She turned away again and Pascal released her hand. She was about to make another choice, take another fork in the road of her life, and, while this one had the potential for so much more pain than Ryan had ever inflicted, it was different this time because she knew this was the right thing. The right choice. It all came down to Pascal and what he would choose, and she couldn't control that.

She took another deep breath and turned to face Pascal again, her eyes roving over his face. Everything about him was so dear to her. So necessary for her well-being. He was looking at her, too, but warily. His expression was guarded again.

With her heart thumping, Alana moved off the seat to kneel before him on the cold stone ground. Pascal reared back, surprised. 'What are you doing?'

Alana rocked back on her heels. 'I'm following my heart, Pascal, but this time I know why I'm doing it and I know it's right—because from the first moment I saw you it's felt right, in here.' Alana put a hand to her belly and then touched her heart. 'And most of all in here. It just took me a while to trust that. To trust myself again.'

Pascal said nothing, but his eyes gleamed with some indefinable emotion and Alana put her trust in that. She took her other hand out of her pocket; it was still clenched over her precious cargo. She looked at Pascal. 'You asked me to consider committing to a life together, to consider that we could try and make things work.'

He cut in harshly. 'I never asked you to marry me, Alana; you've made it abundantly clear how you feel about it. All I wanted was for us to give family life a chance. To give our child a stable foundation.'

'I know,' she said gently. 'And I do want that too.'

He raised an incredulous brow.

She forged on. 'I do, Pascal. But the truth is, I want so much more. I said no to you in Paris, I came back here to try and get some space, because I was afraid of what you were asking, and what might happen if I said yes—that you'd grow tired of me, or take a mistress. I always said I'd never marry again, yet I want to believe in the dream again. And it scares the life out of me, when it had become such a dangerous myth to me. I'd thought I'd given up on that dream for ever.'

She looked back into his eyes, willing him to see what she was feeling, what was in her heart. 'I walked away because deep down I couldn't bear the thought that you didn't love me. I've fallen in love with you, Pascal, and I've realised that I still do want the dream. I can't settle for anything less, no matter how much pain might be in store, even if you say no.' She opened her palm then, and she saw his stricken gaze look down to take in the heavy platinum band nestling there.

'Pascal, I...' God, she couldn't falter now. She kneeled up straighter and held out the ring in her hand, but she could feel it starting to shake. 'Pascal, will you please marry me?'

His eyes met hers, and Alana stopped breathing. Time stopped for an infinitesimal moment and started again in slow, heavy beats and then she realised that it was her heart.

Pascal felt as though a two-tonne lorry had just crashed into his solar plexus. And all he could do was look at her, this woman he loved more than life itself, on her knees in front of him, *proposing* to him. Because she loved him. Finally the momentary shock wore off. He felt a ripple of pure incandescent joy surge upwards through his body. He could see her hand shake, her lips tighten momentarily as if to ward off the inevitable rejection, and ridiculously tears stung the back of his eyes. He was in awe, transfixed by her strength and bravery, and he felt humbled.

He summoned control and held out his left hand. 'I thought you'd never ask.' Alana just stayed there, dumbstruck. Speechless. Pascal fought against tumbling her straight to the ground and kissing her senseless. 'Do you want me to marry you or not?' he said throatily, a smile starting to break through.

She still held back. There was a waver in her husky voice. 'I only want you to marry me if you love me, Pascal.'

His heart ached for her uncertainty, but he had to make her trust just another little bit. To show her trust in him. 'Put the ring on my finger and you'll find out.'

Dammit, couldn't she see? His heart was singing.

With endearing concentration and unbelievable trepidation on her face, Alana took his hand in hers and carefully slid the ring onto his finger. But before she'd even reached the second knuckle he'd pulled her up off her knees and onto his lap. She trusted him, that was all he needed to know.

Alana felt Pascal's arms secure around her waist, and looked down into his eyes. Her world had just been upended. He was shaking his head. 'You put me through hell the last week. You've turned my life inside out and upside down. Letting you walk out of that apartment was the hardest thing I've ever done, but I had to let you go…and I just prayed that you'd come back to me. And you have.'

He reached up a hand and pulled her head down to his, kissing her deeply. Alana was still struggling to get her breath back, still in shock at what she'd just done, at what he'd just said. As if reading her mind, he pulled back before they went up in flames. He smoothed some hair behind one ear and looked into her eyes.

'I love you, Alana. How can you not know that?'

She shook her head faintly; awe made her voice shake. 'I couldn't allow myself to hope it for a second. I knew I had to do this, to tell you how I felt, but I couldn't contemplate your rejection or else I would never have had the guts to tell you.'

He shook his head and pulled her closer. 'I fell in love with you right here, in this stadium. See how I had to come back? It's as if I had to be near the place I saw you first.'

Alana was melting into his warm, strong embrace. She shook her head faintly. 'But how is it possible? It was just an affair.'

His eyes gleamed. 'It was never just an affair. From the moment we first kissed it was more than that. When our eyes met we *knew* each other. We were made for each other.' He smiled then, and it made her chest ache. 'Although, of course, all I saw at the time was you in that shirt and tie, all buttoned up, and all I wanted to do was unbutton you, undo you.'

Alana pushed back to look down at him again, a blush staining her cheeks. 'You undo me every time you look at me.' She caressed his cheek with the back of her hand. Tears stung her eyes; she could feel her lip wobble. She'd come home, finally.

Pascal caught it and wouldn't let her go. 'You do realise that, just because you've put a ring on my finger, you're still going to have to marry me in a church and make an honest man of me?'

She nodded and smiled tremulously, not a hint of her past or any fears in her eyes any more. 'I'm counting on it. I want the world to know you're mine.' Her voice rang with possessiveness, making Pascal's heart sing even more, making his body hum with urgent desire.

He knew now that he could embrace the way she made him feel, knowing that she could contain every part of him, even the part that felt untamed. He knew now that it had just been her instinctive ability to connect with every part of him from the moment they'd met that had unsettled him. He pulled her head back down to his. When they were finally able to stop kissing, Alana sat back and smiled at him shyly. She brought his hand down to cover her belly where their baby was growing strong and bigger every day. 'I have all I need right here, right now. Anything else is a bonus.'

Pascal pulled her head down to his, and just before he kissed her he whispered against her mouth, 'I love you, very much.'

# EPILOGUE

ALANA relaxed back into the luxurious cushions of the huge, comfortable couch. The tiny baby suckling at her breast was inducing a deliciously soporific effect in her blood. A familiar flood of happiness and contentment made her smile as she looked up from her daughter and took in the warmly decorated open-plan sitting room, and the big windows that looked out into a large garden littered with toys. Situated right in the centre of Montmartre, you could be forgiven for thinking you were in the countryside, the hum of Parisian traffic barely discernible through the high trees guarding the property.

This had been one of the first elegantly palatial town houses she and Pascal had looked at that day so long ago, when she'd believed that all he wanted was to set her up in isolated seclusion. When she'd been so confused about how that made her feel. She shook her head mentally at how far removed that image was from the reality of their life now.

Her heart rate zinged up a notch when a familiar scent teased her nostrils and the couch dipped beside her. As if sensing her father's presence, Orla's head jerked away from Alana's breast, big, brown eyes opening to seek him out. Pascal came close and kissed the baby's head before nuzzling a kiss to Alana's neck, making exquisite shards of desire race through her blood. She marvelled that even while she was breastfeeding, with her baby belly still evident, Pascal's attraction for her didn't seem to diminish. It was the most heady feeling. It got even more heady when he growled into her ear, 'How is it that I can be jealous of my own daughter?'

Alana turned her head to meet his mouth in a brief, searing kiss and then said dryly, 'Well, it's not as if you haven't been through this before; I'm sure you'll survive.' Pascal smiled wolfishly, but then took Orla from Alana to place her on his shoulder and pat her back with all the dexterity of someone well practised in the art. Just then the fruits of his earlier practising efforts exploded into the room.

They were two black-haired, dark-eyed miniature versions of Pascal, one slightly smaller than the other. They were both pulling at a green rugby jersey emblazoned with the Ireland logo. The taller one wailed, 'Papa, it's my turn to wear the Ireland jersey, I don't want to be French today, tell Sam it's his turn to be French. Anyway, it's too big for him!'

The smaller of the two boys clinging desperately to the jersey—three-year-old Samir, named after his paternal grandfather—stood with a bottom lip quivering and tears glistening on ridiculously long lashes.

Pascal shot a wryly accusing look to Alana, whose mouth was twitching as she unsuccessfully held in a grin. She looked at him reproachfully, 'What? You knew I came from a large family.'

'Yes, but that's not it,' he said with mock severity. 'Do we have to encourage our sons to support either one country or the other?'

Alana started to do up her bra and shirt and stood up from the couch, looking down at her husband sprawled before her with Orla successfully burped and falling asleep contentedly on his shoulder.

With her hands on the buttons of her shirt, and seeing the way Pascal's eyes were lingering there explicitly, she valiantly ignored his look and said, 'On the day of the Six Nations match between Ireland and France? It's only natural that our eldest, most discerning son will want to support the team about to win a Grand Slam. And don't blame me for their competitive streak; I think we can safely say they got that from you.'

She flashed him a cheeky grin and turned to go and deal with her sons' spat, but Pascal grabbed her wrist and she laughingly fell back as he pulled her onto his lap and claimed her mouth for a kiss.

On cue, the two boys forgot all about the rugby jersey and started making loud vomiting noises. 'Ugh! Gross!' declared Patrick as he dragged his younger brother away. 'You two better not get all kissy at the match. *So* not cool.'

Alana finally pulled away breathlessly and smiled into Pascal's face. She imitated Patrick. '*So* not cool, but *so* much fun.'

'Hmm,' murmured Pascal appreciatively, settling Alana into one arm while holding Orla with the other. 'Have I told you yet today how much I love you, Mme Lévêque?'

She lifted her head to look at him and smiled coquettishly, running a finger down his chest. 'I don't believe you have, M Lévêque, but you could make it up to me.'

'How?'

Alana pretended to think for a second, her head on one side. 'Let me see. As our lovely nanny has offered to babysit tonight, you could take me out for dinner….'

His eyes darkened and she felt his body grow taut underneath her. 'Anywhere in mind?' he asked with a gruff tone, vivid images already filling his head.

'Oh, I'm sure I can think of somewhere…' Alana came close and pressed a kiss to his mouth '…nice and cosy.' She moved down and pressed another kiss to his neck where his pulse beat fast. 'Somewhere intimate…private…'

'Where we won't be disturbed?' His voice became gruffer.

She pulled back and looked at him, and smiled, her eyes shining with love for him.

'My thoughts exactly.'

Pascal felt his daughter squirm slightly against his shoulder, and felt his wife wriggle on his lap, making lust arrow straight to his groin. He heard the scuffle of his two sons playing nearby, and his heart swelled in his chest. The moment was huge, buoyant, and though his life was filled with such moments now, this didn't diminish it in any way. Alana just looked at him with innate understanding in her eyes. She smiled and said simply, 'I know—and I love you, too.'

And that was all that needed to be said.

# ⟐ MILLS & BOON®
### *Pure reading pleasure*™

## FEBRUARY 2009 HARDBACK TITLES

# ROMANCE

| | |
|---|---|
| The Spanish Billionaire's Pregnant Wife | Lynne Graham |
| The Italian's Ruthless Marriage Command | Helen Bianchin |
| The Brunelli Baby Bargain | Kim Lawrence |
| The French Tycoon's Pregnant Mistress | Abby Green |
| Forced Wife, Royal Love-Child | Trish Morey |
| The Rich Man's Blackmailed Mistress | Robyn Donald |
| Pregnant with the De Rossi Heir | Maggie Cox |
| The British Billionaire's Innocent Bride | Susanne James |
| The Timber Baron's Virgin Bride | Daphne Clair |
| The Magnate's Marriage Demand | Robyn Grady |
| Diamond in the Rough | Diana Palmer |
| Secret Baby, Surprise Parents | Liz Fielding |
| The Rebel King | Melissa James |
| Nine-to-Five Bride | Jennie Adams |
| Marrying the Manhattan Millionaire | Jackie Braun |
| The Cowboy and the Princess | Myrna Mackenzie |
| The Midwife and the Single Dad | Gill Sanderson |
| The Playboy Firefighter's Proposal | Emily Forbes |

# HISTORICAL

| | |
|---|---|
| The Disgraceful Mr Ravenhurst | Louise Allen |
| The Duke's Cinderella Bride | Carole Mortimer |
| Impoverished Miss, Convenient Wife | Michelle Styles |

# MEDICAL™

| | |
|---|---|
| A Family For His Tiny Twins | Josie Metcalfe |
| One Night with Her Boss | Alison Roberts |
| Top-Notch Doc, Outback Bride | Melanie Milburne |
| A Baby for the Village Doctor | Abigail Gordon |